PENGUIN BOOKS

A SINLESS SEASON

Damon Galgut was born in 1963 in Pretoria, South Africa.
He attended Pretoria Boys' High School where he was head
boy in 1981. His one-act play, 'No 1, Utopia Lane', won
the 1981 Pretoria Play Festival for High Schools which was
organized by the South African Council for English Education. He also won the Argus Group's Short Story compe-
tition in 1981. In 1980 he was placed third in the Rank
Xerox English Olympiad for which he won an overseas
trip. His first two-act play, 'Echoes of Anger', was produced by the Performing Arts Council of the Transvaal
who also produced his second play, 'Alive and Kicking', in
1984. On the completion of his National Service commitment he was appointed the first resident playwright for the
Performing Arts Council of the Transvaal, a position which
he still holds. *A Sinless Season* is his first novel.

DAMON GALGUT

A SINLESS SEASON

PENGUIN BOOKS

Penguin Books Ltd, Harmondsworth, Middlesex, England
Penguin Books, 40 West 23rd Street, New York, New York 10010, U.S.A.
Penguin Books Australia Ltd, Ringwood, Victoria, Australia
Penguin Books Canada Ltd, 2801 John Street, Markham, Ontario, Canada L3R 1B4
Penguin Books (N.Z.) Ltd, 182-190 Wairau Road, Auckland 10, New Zealand

First published by Jonathan Ball Publishers 1982
Published in Penguin Books 1984

Made and printed in Great Britain by
Richard Clay (The Chaucer Press) Ltd, Bungay, Suffolk
Set in Times

I would like to express my thanks to two groups of people who have stood by me in my writing. The first is my family, the most supportive members of which have been my parents and my grandmother, Mrs Rose Fisher. The other is my friends, of whom there are too many who have lent aid for me to name them individually. I single out only one: Laetitia Lynch, a lady of the richest quality, to whom I can never repay what I owe. She has only the very meagre acknowledgement of my deep love and gratitude.

For Dean Fourie and David Lord

...forgive me
For the sins that in me the world shall commit, my words
when they speak me, my thoughts when they think me,
my treason engendered by traitors beyond me,
my life when they murder by means of my
hands, my death when they live me.

from 'Prayer before Birth'
by Louis Macneice

Action is transitory – a step, a blow,
The motion of a muscle – this way or that –
'Tis done, and in the after-vacancy
We wonder at ourselves like men betrayed:
Suffering is permanent, obscure and dark,
And shares the nature of infinity.

from 'The Borderers'
by William Wordsworth

PART I

Those moments that live inside us for ever...

Scott Berry paused at the foot of the entrance stair and turned back his eyes on the margin of a continent. Wind rumpled his hair. At the fringe of the slopes pouring down from the road Raoul's tiny figure seemed lost in an immensity of sea and sky. He was staring down at the water.

'Come, Raoul,' Scott called. 'They're waiting for us.'

His voice, whether unheard or unheeded, had no effect. Scott had again that sense of being almost a physical anachronism in his circumstances; an Aeneas in a metaphorical underworld. How much more than just two years, he wondered, had he sacrificed by his actions?

Slowly he dropped his bags to the tarmac and crossed over to Raoul. They stood, side by side, gazing down the medley of cliffs and peaks to where the sea simmered hundreds of feet below. Distantly, a gull cried.

'The sea here looks different to what it does at New Baytown,' Scott said.

After a few seconds Raoul murmured, 'Like it?'

'Looks ... like iron.'

'What did they say it symbolizes?'

'The sea? Eternity. The sea symbolizes eternity.'

Looking at this shivering and battered sheet of aluminium foil, Scott could indeed glimpse something unending in the infinity of waves. Although he did not speak, a turmoil of unuttered words filled his mind. He had felt this way all through the drive to Bleda and beyond, along the further five kilometre stretch of coastal road. Even now, the recollection of his pale face, reflected like a candle flame in the car window, was very strong ... and also what he associated with it.

Repulsion?

No – and yes, in an uncomfortable sense: staring at his own

flesh and knowing that it was simply a housing for feeling. A generator of emotion. No more, no less.

Raoul spoke again.

'Scott, there are bars on the windows,' he said.

Scott looked up at the fiercely impassive facade behind them and saw the cold slats. Dropping his gaze, he saw too that the doors were heavy and hinged with steel, but he said nothing. This was their home for the next two years and it does not do to fear one's home.

'Of course,' he said. 'They have to have them.'

Raoul nodded heavily, but his eyes were not on the building, or on Scott. They burned down onto the water, watching the waves.

Not able to move his gaze from the grey stonework, Scott was conscious of the attractive memories painted through his brain; the beautiful and idyllic in all that was familiar. All that he had left behind. All that he had given up. For what? For this? For a comfortless fortress stored with reprimand, and a sky made more dead by the hollow calls of gulls?

Whatever its site, whatever its success, Scott feared it.

'Come on, you guys,' Joseph Hamilton shouted from the stairs. 'They're waiting for us.'

Somnambulists in a sleepless realm, they began to walk back towards the entrance.

Eugene Hall, principal of Bleda Reformatory, appraised the faces of the three boys in front of him with a single brief glance. He was not by nature a man given to brief glances, but many years devoted to intense reformation of errant youth had changed much in his nature. Indeed, he lived now by conventions that would have been alien to him while he was one of their number. All three of them were staring at him with belligerent eyes.

Joseph Hamilton was not, Mr Hall decided, the leader of this trio. Plump and dark, with grainy, unsubtle features, there was a nervousness to be detected in the restless clasp of his hands and the unsettled pulse of his stare.

Scott Berry – hardly the stock criminal figure, Mr Hall observed. Sensitive brown eyes, chestnut hair, arched black eyebrows, an aquiline nose. There was an air of meekness about him – misleading? – or was it suggested by the diffident calm of that face? Once again Mr Hall wondered whether it was possible to find the criminal in man by examining his expression.

Last in the sweep of Mr Hall's glance, yet largest in his scrutiny, came Raoul Dean. Almost sixteen years of age, Raoul had the stature and casual indifference of a ten year old. His crown of ebony curls, which topped a snub-nosed, dark-eyed face that was steeped in innocence, reached only to Scott's shoulder. This slightness was uniform throughout his body; his wrists and torso were slim. Mr Hall wondered.

The appraisal, however, was a mutual one. The three youths made quiet private decisions about this grey-haired, balding man in a sober blue suit. For each, he represented a first glimpse of the inhabitants of this unencountered world.

'Please sit down,' Mr Hall said, motioning at the chairs in front of his desk. 'Welcome,' he continued, 'to Bleda. I don't like to call it a reformatory – I'm sure you'll agree that's neither a nice word, nor a fair one.' He paused, breathing through his mouth. The whole speech was musty with practice, he could hear it himself. It was the same one he made to all newcomers. 'There are, fortunately, fewer than one hundred people here. Their ages range from ten to twenty-one. The building was erected in 1927, which makes it thirty-four years old. I want to reassure you that the bars on the windows date from those early years – we do not maintain such standards of security today.' He smiled. 'In fact, we have no standards at all. You are allowed to walk around the grounds as you please, when you please. We trust you.'

They waited as Mr Hall scrabbled a cigarette from his pocket and poised it between his lips. While he rasped a match alight, he continued to speak from the corner of his mouth.

'You are allowed to ... um, I said that ... We trust you.' Smoke scrolled up across his face. 'I must impress certain things on you, though. Remember, we have pride here. That is why we do not call this a reformatory. This is a school, like any other, and you are boys, like any others. Let me be frank with you – other reformatories would treat you like criminals. But not here. We have managed to turn our boys into gentlemen. We hope to do the same to you. You will be struck by the decency of the boys here – there is no coarseness. We expect the same from you. No swearing, bullying, that sort of thing. Do you understand me?'

The response: three unsmiling nods. Mr Hall drew on the cigarette.

'I understand your present feelings,' he said after a while. 'But it has been decided that you be sent here to us. If your attitude is correct from the very beginning, I promise you that you will actually enjoy your stay. You will learn many things.'

Raoul tried to yawn tiredly. Ignoring him, Mr Hall dragged a heavy black book across the desk and thumbed it open.

'I have read Mr Chesselet's report on your home circumstances. I have read the records of your trial and Justice van der Westhuizen's judgement. You are, all of you, on police record. You have been following a misguided course. I understand that your first crime was one of shoplifting; charges were not pressed, is that right?' Scott nodded as Mr Hall's eyes found his face. 'Your second crime was one of attempted theft. You all three ran away from home before the day you were supposed to appear in court. On being recaptured, you were taken to face a children's court and each received four strokes with a light cane. Immediately afterward, you ran away from home for a second time, but not before assaulting the probation officer appointed to investigate your case. Is all of this correct?'

Scott knew that Mr Hall was fully aware of the accuracy of his account. He had a deep urge to explain himself, to lay claim to innate sensitivity and pain, but he said nothing. He nodded across the desk. Mr Hall, tapping ash from his cigarette, went on.

'All of you are, at present, under sixteen years of age.' It was a statement. 'You are therefore obliged to remain here until you turn eighteen. The dates for your respective releases stand at, Scott – 20th of April, 1963; Joseph – 18th of November, 1963; and Raoul – 13th of September, 1963.' He paused again, still looking down at the page. Scott noticed the thin strands combed over the top of his head, the scalp daubed pinkly here and there. Then the face came up, the cigarette hanging limp.

'In theory,' he said. 'That is purely in theory. In practice, you can make it much easier for yourselves. We encourage you to.' Another silence. 'Are you familiar with the licence system?'

'No,' said Raoul.

'By licence in writing the management of this institution is entitled to permit you to live in the custody of a suitable person.'

'For how long?' Raoul asked, a sudden new ember lighting his eyes. Mr Hall, surprised at this unexpected response, tried to warm himself on it.

'For as long as we decide,' he said. 'Provided it does not exceed two years, or, obviously, extend beyond the time you have been sentenced for. The time can be drawn out for longer than two years with the Minister's permission only. That will hardly be necessary in your cases, however. We will require you to spend a fair amount of time here, so that we may observe your conduct.' Thin lips chipped a smile out of his face. 'So, if you decide to co-operate, life will not prove to be overly bleak.'

Scott dropped his eyes for the first time.

'I am allowed, too,' continued Mr Hall, 'to grant you leave of absence for certain periods of time. If, for any reason, you should require such leave, I want you to feel free to come and discuss it with me.'

'Does this also mean for visiting people?' Raoul asked.

'It does. Naturally, we cannot grant such leave immediately. Again, you will have to stay here for a certain amount of time before such freedom can be given. You do understand that?'

Strong sunlight notched the shape of leaves on the far wall, trembling in an unfelt breeze.

'Discharge can also be brought into effect. Not often, but it is possible. The Minister would of course have to discuss such a matter with me first. If I believe that discharge would be reasonable, the Minister has the authority to order it. By the same token, if I believe that a longer period of retention is necessary, that can also be arranged. Your fate,' he smiled reassuringly, 'rests with me. Impress me and you won't regret it. Distress me, and ...' His fingers tapped a warning on the table-top. It was the threat of society.

They waited. The leaves on the wall were still now, steady as bayonets. Mr Hall sat back in his chair, his fingers moving on the buttons of his shirt front.

'You will find,' he said, 'that education here is geared towards the mechanical, the industrial side of things. Intensely so. Our teachers are few. If you find it difficult to adjust, come and speak to me. I doubt that you will, however; very few people do. The matron will show you up to your dormitory and –' he flung a glance at his watch – 'in forty-five minutes the boys will be up from class. I have informed them of your arrival and no doubt they will help you into the routine. I wish you luck. One other thing – you must report to roll-call in our upstairs lounge every evening at 5.50 pm. This is really the only check we keep on you. Now remember what I said about a tradition of turning out young gentlemen.' He rose abruptly behind his desk and stood still.

Confused, the boys got to hesitant feet, then started for the door. As they reached it, a cocker spaniel yawned beneath the desk, raising an indolent head.

Mr Hall laughed, gestured to the warm room, lined with book-cases, thickly carpeted, immaculately painted, then dropped his hand to the dog. 'Completes the image of homeliness,' he said.

The boys smiled politely and moved through the doorway. Scott Berry suppressed his inner trembling, forced strength into his weak hands, and turned the handle behind him. Homeliness. Was that what they called it? It was totally foreign to him.

The dormitory was large, with rows of neat beds down each wall. From the far window, open to the sun, Scott could see the vast desolation of blue water, becoming paler, faded, as it neared its indistinguishable seam with the sky. The day was windless now, objects waxing and waning in the fuming air. He rested his chin on the sill.

'Have you seen the *bathroom*?' Raoul said, his small head appearing round the doorway which led off to the right. Joseph looked up from his suitcase.

'Come unpack, Raoul,' he said, hauling a mound of clothes onto his bed.

'Whafor? Have you seen the bathroom? In there. Whatcha looking at, Scottie?'

'Sea.'

'Whafor? Jesus, they've done this place up inside, hey. Looks real shit from outside. There aren't no bars on this window. Maybe they didn't put them on the second floor rooms. Watcha looking at, Scott?'

Scott felt hard iron stubs along the base of the window frame. 'There were bars,' he said. 'Sawn off.'

'Is it? Let me see.' He stepped up as Scott moved aside. 'Yes, bars once. Hey, did you get a load of that old screwball with the fancy words? No swearing, my arse. Is he mad?'

'You guys better unpack,' Joseph said. 'The others will be up here soon.'

'Jesus, I could care.' Raoul jumped down and sprawled on his bed.

'How many are there?'

8

'Count the beds,' Joseph suggested, closing his locker on the contents of his suitcase and turning the key in the lock.

'Hey, Scottie, have you seen the *bathroom*?'

'Where?'

'Come, I'll show you.' Raoul bounced noisily off the bed to the door. 'They've really done it up inside.'

Scott followed him down two shallow steps into a long low room, tiled in pale blue. It had obviously been newly refitted, for the floor was relatively unsullied and the towel racks were gleaming. Three separate shower booths were ranged down the length of the room, divided by thin walls. At the far end were two baths, and to the left of the entrance a short wing with toilets and basins. Scott began to walk, his footsteps quavering coldly off the walls.

'Bloody nice, huh, Scottie? Bloody nice. How much was all this, d'you think? Bloody fortune, I'll tell you that.' Raoul darted into one of the showers and tried the water. He came out seconds later, hand dripping. 'Hot water too. How often do we get to shower?'

Scott reached the baths and tested their depth. Then he began to walk back. Raoul was pulling a shower curtain to and fro, looking up in apparent fascination at the brass rings on the supporting bar. Scott passed him and moved out into the dormitory again.

'You better unpack, Scott,' Joseph told him, lying shoeless on his bed. 'It's getting fucking late.'

'Whassa time?' Raoul asked, reappearing from the cloak-room. 'Stop ratting 'bout how late it is, Joe. You're getting on my tit.'

'Christ, you can talk; you not exactly –'

'Hey, Scottie, anything happening out there? You see anything?'

'Nothing, Raoul.'

'Ahh, Jesus, what happens in this joint? I haven't got any smokes. Didja bring smokes, Joe?'

Scott, leaning on the window-sill again, rooted his mind in distance. Far below him a path ran like discarded hemp through the trees, becoming unseen as it neared the drop to the sea. There all sight was patterned by broken shards of colour – the glint of a beach, the muddy stains of shadow, a white pucker of foam. Scott leaned forward, puzzled. From between the clenched knees of two nearby mountains, a spear of brown water was thrust into the ocean, dissolving five hundred metres out in the bay. He stared at it, mystified.

'Christ, what a crappy place for a bed.' Raoul opened his case and punched his clothes with a fist. 'You gonna unpack, Scottie? The others will be coming up now.'

Joseph belched resoundingly.

'Joe, you bloody pig! Haven't you got culture?'

'Bugger you.'

'My dear sir,' Raoul said, laying out handfuls of clothes in the drawers of his locker, 'my breeding does not permit me to associate with you.' He brightened. 'Hey, didja hear that old coot with the fancy words this morning? "You will find that education here is geared..." Jesus, I ask you. Is he mad?'

'Scott, you better come unpack.' Joseph raised himself on his elbows. 'What are you looking at?'

'Hey, Scottie, you bring any smokes? I forgot–'

'Ahh, leave off with the smokes, huh, Raoul?' Joseph heaved himself to his feet and moved over to the cloakroom door, unzipping his fly. 'I need a leak.'

Raoul jumped over the bed. 'Have you seen the *bathroom*, Joe? Come, I'll show you.' He followed him inside. Silence set like hard crystal in the room, freezing objects into its rigid heart. Scott stared, unmoving.

'When do we get to shower?' Raoul asked, bounding into the dormitory again. 'Huh, Scottie?'

Scott shrugged, chin burrowing into the warm window-sill. Raoul sat down on his bed and tugged a shoe loose. 'You reckon I can shower now?' he demanded. Scott shrugged again.

Joseph emerged, zipping up his fly. 'Watcha doing, Raoul?' he asked suspiciously.

'I'm gonna shower, Fatso. Mind?' Raoul threw his shirt

down across the bed and pulled at his belt.

'You haven't finished unpacking yet,' Joseph said. 'The others'll be coming up soon.'

'I could care.' Stepping out of his pants, Raoul sorted a towel from the tangle of clothes on his bed. 'I wanna shower now.'

Scott turned at the window and looked down. Sunlight crisped the smooth planes of Raoul's face, gilding with fine wire the deep angelic eyes, smiling now; the well-defined curve of the brows; the firm and emotionless mouth. There was a pause as they stared at one another.

'My nakedness shames me,' Raoul said, stepping through the doorway into the cloakroom. Joseph and Scott remained as they were – carved forms – while the sound of water bursting on tiles came flowing over them. Day lay heavily on the earth.

'So what's it with you?' Joseph said, pillowing his head on his hands. 'You depressed, or what?'

'What's that brown part of the sea there?' Scott asked, pointing out of the window. Joseph yawned widely.

'Dunno,' he said. 'Probably rocks. Rocks everywhere here. Hey, how many people are there in this place?'

Scott shrugged once more, slitting his eyes against the white gusts of sunlight.

'Yes, but like how many d'you *think*?'

Raoul shouted from the adjoining room. 'Hey there, this is bee-yoo-ti-ful! Come on, Fatso, you can't believe this. Do we get to shower every day?'

'Shuddup,' Joseph replied in an undertone. 'There's quite a few beds in here,' he observed.

'Hey, come and shower, you guys! This is bee-yoo-ti-ful!'

'We hear you, okay!'

'Shutup, Fatso.'

Joseph and Scott became simultaneously aware of a presence occupying the doorway to the dormitory. There was another drenching silence as words became ill-placed, hanging in the spaces between them.

Scott had never thought he would come across one of his

peers who was shorter than Raoul. The person regarding them at the present moment was shorter and smaller – in all senses smaller – than Raoul Dean. His rich brown hair, lightly curling at the ears, framed a face epitomizing the benign innocence of the cherub, down to the wide smile and fine smattering of freckles; but this image was curiously belied by the slimness of his body, the china-fragility of his crossed-arm pose in the doorway.

The boys continued to stare for ten shell-shocked seconds, the room almost trembling in the concussion of this silent meeting.

'You still there?' Raoul demanded from the adjoining room.

'You are the new boys,' the vision declared slowly, with the air of one drawing a final and well-considered conclusion. There was no reply. After a pause, the speaker detached himself from the jamb, in much the same way that a young child might pluck a petal from a flower, and drifted into the room.

'My name is Anthony Lord,' he said.

'Scottie ... Joe – are you still there?'

'I'm Scott Berry.' Scott moved down the room and met the extended hand. Anthony Lord's grip was warm and firm. Scott found himself looking into the crystalline depths of two blue eyes. 'Pleased to meet you,' he said.

'I'm Joe Hamilton.' Another handshake followed. As he moved back against a bed, Scott became acutely conscious of the texture of the sheets beneath his hands. He had played over in his mind the many possible variations of his first encounter with this unknown world, but none as farcical as this had raised itself into his imagination. The words of Eugene Hall rose like stirred dust into his mind: '...you will be struck by the decency of the boys here. There is no coarseness...'

Raoul Dean appeared in the cloakroom door, drying his sodden hair. As his eyes fell on the newcomer, he became rigid. Then he dropped his hands to his sides, holding the towel across his lower body. 'Hello,' he said.

'My name is Anthony Lord,' the distinctive voice declared

again. Words seemed to shred in lazy haste from his mouth, blurred with the same sense of hushed urgency that pervaded his slowest movement. Raoul shook the proferred hand tentatively, clenching the towel about his waist at his left hip. There was an uneasy pause.

'The others will be coming up now,' Anthony Lord informed them, clambering onto one of the beds and crossing his legs, Buddha-style. 'I'm early.'

'I haven't finished unpacking yet.' Scott took his avenue of escape, moving back down to his suitcase.

'Nor me.' Raoul made several bounds down the row of beds, scattering water like chips of broken glass. Just briefly, Scott glimpsed something ... reverent ... sacred ... in the moment: the open window burning white sunlight in a translucent aura about Raoul's silhouetted body.

Joseph Hamilton began to pick his nose.

All four of them sensed rather than heard the deep tremor of a bell in the building below them; a heartbeat in the stone. Movement, suddenly, was too casual – waiting. Even Anthony Lord turned his head to one side and gazed intently at the door.

At first there was no response to the summons of sound and will. And then, distantly, like the lonely whistle of a long-awaited train in the night, footsteps thudded in broken cavalcade; a linoleum overture ... to what? Scott frantically stuffed the last handful of clothing into his drawer and closed the locker. He breathed deeply.

'We'll go swimming this afternoon,' Anthony told them, his stare fixed once again on their part of the room. 'It's hot today.'

They nodded agreement, feeling foolish. Still they waited, avoiding each others' gazes, mouths papery and dry. Scott tried to control the feathery blinking of his eyes.

Louder now, the ordered clip of many walking feet swelled in the corridor outside. At last, all sight in the room was openly centred on that door. The contact was about to take place – that initial dreaded collision with the faceless archangels of cruelty and mindlessness. No one took breath.

In the doorway a neatly dressed, short-haired individual hesitated. 'Hello there,' he said at last, his voice rich and easy with warmth. 'You're the new ones, hey?' He grinned broadly, holding out his hand. 'I'm Martin Everitt. Been here long? Sorry we were a while – school, you know.' He shook hands with Joseph. 'Hope you won't find it hard to settle in with us disagreeable blokes.'

Scott watched numbly as Martin came across the room to shake his hand in greeting. Behind him, fifteen other boys trooped in, all neat, with short hair and pleasant faces. All welcomed them with feeling; all were genuinely concerned as to their comfort. It seemed that the whole room was fluttering with levity. Sentences buffeted him from all sides. 'I'm Mark.' … 'Have you had a chance to unpack yet?'…'My name is Spencer Hardy'…'Hot today, eh?'…'My name is Craig Draper'…'Have you met Mr Hall?'…'My name is…'…'I'm Chris Murray'…'Is there anything you need?'…'I'm…'…'My name is…'…'My name is…'

Scott felt himself becoming physically relaxed. The claims of Bleda Reformatory were not far-fetched, it appeared. Up till that time the prospect of returning to his home had been an inviting one. Now, however, it began to stale when viewed comparatively. He could survive. He could live here for two years.

'Soon,' Spencer Hardy told him, 'we'll all go down for lunch. I'll introduce you to Mr Bishop then – quite a nice old bod. After that we'll be allowed to go down to the beach to swim. It's pretty hot today.' Scott nodded dumbly, unable to reply.

'Have you been around the grounds yet?' Mark Archer enquired of him. 'They're quite extensive, really. They stretch down to the sea. I'm told we own a piece of the beach too – that bit you can see here, from the cliffs on the right, up to –'

'What's that brown part of the sea there?' Scott asked, pointing into the white glare off the water. 'You can't really see it now, though.'

14

'Yes, I know where you mean. It's from a river that flows down there. We sometimes swim in it, but we shouldn't. You never know what they dump into the water higher upstream.'

There was a break in their conversation. Looking down onto the platter of lawn adjoining the building, Scott recognized Mr Hall's spaniel trotting beside the flowerbeds, nose to the ground. It stopped and raised its head. The sound of sharp barking drifted up to them.

'I'll kill that animal one day,' Mark vowed. 'It barks without stopping.'

'Tell me,' Scott said, unsure of himself. 'I ... you...'

'What?'

'Are you guys always like this?'

'Always like what?'

'Like ... this.' A helpless shrug.

'Don't know what you mean.'

'For better or worse,' Chris Murray remarked in passing, 'we are always like this. Whatever that might hold for you.' He smiled.

Scott leaned forward across the sill and expelled his breath lightly from between his lips. The lazy air resisted the movement, but teasingly so; it lay warm as mud across his face. All at once Scott lived a moment of absolute joy – the afternoon and a promise of eternal afternoons like this, strummed airy fingers across his mind. There had been too much sadness, too much fear, in a past too tenuous to bear what it had to, for any prospect of peace to lie in the future. He tapped a ditty with his fingers and glanced at Raoul.

He was instantly afraid.

For Scott, looking at Raoul had always been an action far transcending the immediate. His eyes seemed to paste Raoul's figure with images recalled or anticipated, images that generated unaccountable shiftings of nervousness in the heart. One lived a lifetime in such a glance. Scott knew Raoul well, was absolutely familiar with details and perspectives of his body and face – strangely familiar, he often thought. Sometimes a vision of startling clarity would come to Scott when he least expected it. He would find his mind immersed in a close scrutiny of the veins which ran through Raoul's neck, or discover himself staring mentally into those restless, dark eyes. Later it would come to him as a shock that these were details he had not in actuality noticed, although they were real. He knew things about Raoul, he sometimes thought, without having seen them for himself.

And yet, at other times, there was a space where recollection should be. More than once over the last period, when Scott's dreams were riddled with torment over the direction of his life, he had woken in the night and found he could not picture Raoul's face. He would sit and press his palms into his eyes with furious passion, but the figure he remembered remained faceless and distant. Such times terrified Scott, the more so because he could not understand his need to recall the face that had ruined all promise that life held for him.

This need, however, had always seemed symptomatic of a far more powerful obsession. The instant that Scott had set eyes on Raoul had been one that he seemed to have lived with all his life. He had heard people speak of walking into an unfamiliar place and knowing that they had been there before in dreams or lives past. Such a sensation had gripped Scott upon meeting Raoul. Then, however, it was not the surroundings that seemed familiar but something else ... the time? The feelings inside his head? The presence of Raoul Dean?

Scott shook free of this troubling speculation and returned to a window-sill in Bleda Reformatory. His skin was numbed with warmth. Turning, he had to screw up his eyes to let them grow accustomed to the shade of the room's interior. Already most of the boys were trooping down to lunch. Scott caught sight of Anthony Lord in the doorway; he walked with extended paces that made their own tacit mockery of his stature.

Raoul was the last to leave. He went alone, head tilted forward on his shoulders, one hand trailing absently along the wall. Scott listened emptily to the slow thud of the clock above his bed until the footfalls had drained away. He counted off sixty seconds to amuse himself, then stood and crossed to the

cloakroom door. As he was about to enter he caught sight of
Spencer Hardy standing in the middle of the floor. Scott
opened his mouth to make comment, but the air turned
soundless between his lips as he stared.

Spencer Hardy was clearly not aware of Scott's presence.
He stood shirtless in front of a washbasin mirror and grinned
at his reflection. He flexed the muscles of his chest and studied the twitching of his sinews in the glass. He patted the
smooth skin of his shoulders and face with pride. He winked
at himself and sighed with pleasure.

'You're strong,' said Spencer Hardy to himself.

Scott held the towel across his shoulders, feeling the weight of
the meal in his belly. The food had been good beyond expectation; a full richness of taste still lingered in his mouth. He
had so much feared a frugal Oliver Twist fare that the gener-
ous and wholesome reality gave strength to the inanity of the
illusions he had held. Hell lay only beyond the perimeter of
Bleda Reformatory.

He, together with Raoul and Joe, was part of a larger group
from their dormitory going down to the beach. Anticipation
of a swim and a chance to relax in the sun had given Scott a
happy lightness of mood. He was almost looking forward to
finding his feet in this ordered and civilized society.

The path that he had seen from above was the one that they
now took to the beach. It lay at a slight slope down from the
lawn, blued with dappled shadow from the huge pines about
them. The air, thick with the sweet scent of resin, trembled
with their soft conversation. They moved in file and Scott saw
before him the chestnut hair and jutting ears of Anthony
Lord. Light tattooed him in liquid puddles as he walked.

From the belt of pines the path cut its way along a broad
shelf that rested near the crest of a hill. Vague in the shifting
shadows of the woods, the ground pillared away to their right;
some distance away on the other hand, the lip of a cliff was
drawn like a bright cord. As the slope steepened, the cliff

drew nearer to them until they stepped into a wash of brilliant sunlight and wind, with the drop plunging sheer on their left.

'Always be careful when you come up here,' Spencer Hardy told them. 'This is an extremely dangerous part of the path.'

In a long row they gazed out over the bay. At their feet the cliff sheered away for two hundred heady feet, choked at its base with a gnarled smoke of trees. It was countered by a featureless blue headland that obtruded at the far side of the two kilometre stretch of beach. Between these outstretched arms the sand rolled like a motionless golden sea, freckled already with the figures of recumbent boys.

From that point the path scribbled down a shoulder of land, between boulders and steamy runs of forest. They walked in file once more, negotiating with difficulty the drops and slides that pocked their way. At last the path flowed down a cool channel carved through the high tides of greenery on either side, and spilled onto the beach.

Standing in the fine bleached sand that whitewashed the coastline, Scott smelt the hard salty tang of the sea. He could almost not bring himself to move as he looked out upon the water, so close now that the burst and hiss of the waves lay all about him like the wind. He gripped the ends of the towel tightly in both hands.

'The sea is never, always, and for ever; it is eternal, and the sea is eternity.'

The voice seemed to be a whisper from his own consciousness. Shocked, he turned his head. Anthony Lord stood at his side, gazing past the horizons that bound him, and Scott saw the sightlessness of flint in his eyes. Then he moved his head with birdlike swiftness and smiled up at Scott. There was a sad gaiety in that smile; laughter paints its lines like cracked and fading plaster. They fell into step across the beach.

'What did you say?'

'Just talking.' Anthony smiled again.

Their footsteps crunched in unison across the sand. Looking about him, Scott recognized many of the faces he had seen in the dining-room; many young, few older than himself. Mr Bishop, whom he had already met, was standing atop a small rise, hands on hips. He looked down and nodded.

'Hey, Scottie, have you seen the *sea*?' Raoul bounded up, flicking his towel at the sand. 'Come on, I'll take you swimming.'

'In a minute, Raoul. Just hang on.'

As if it were the habit of many years, Scott, Raoul and Anthony laid their towels in a row on the sand. They stood, again side by side, Scott in the centre, facing the curve of the sea. Across the bay to the right the extended bluff seemed drunkenly suspended, a black marble limb floating in the shimmering water. Anthony pointed out beyond its tip.

'You can see forever,' he said.

Scott followed the pointing finger with his eyes.

The sea extended hazily into the paleness of infinity. Scott turned his eyes back to Anthony, but he had gone, running down the firm slope of the beach toward the sea.

Raoul stood up from the dragging sand with a violent heave. He had been lying so long that the muscles in his body were limp with drowsiness. Slapping grit from his arms, he looked around him.

Less than half the number of boys who had originally come down to the beach were left now. Although it was already mid-afternoon the foliage of the surrounding forest sent giddy waves of heat up into the air so that the lines of the hilltops wavered and shook. Raoul moved three quick paces to the cool brown of wave-washed sand.

He could see Scott out in the bay, beyond the surf. He was sitting on the crest of a large sandbank which scraped at the surface of the sea. There was another small figure with him. Raoul shaded his eyes with a carefully bent hand and squinted. It took him a few seconds to recognise Anthony Lord. He and Scott were sitting together, it seemed without talking, while the water rushed softly in a bubbling skin over the sand between them. Raoul watched them for a while longer, then dropped his hand and began to trot along the beach.

Scott could pick out Raoul's figure even from that distance. He knew the careful carriage of Raoul's upper body, the contrivedly uncontrived swinging of his thin arms. He considered shouting to him, but decided not to. Something in the disturbingly silent poise of Anthony Lord forbade such an action. Scott kept his eyes fixedly ahead of him. He had looked over only once when Anthony had arrived, breaking sudden as a seal from the blue water. Although they were only two metres apart the dark form of the sandbank dissolved into nothing. It seemed as though Anthony, in that distinctive Buddha style, was sitting on top of the supporting sea. So Scott looked straight ahead of him and followed Raoul's path across the sand.

It took only half a minute before Raoul's steady jog carried him from the oppressive closeness of the group. He preferred to be alone and in motion, not allowing his body to solidify into the restrictions of companionship or stillness. Now he felt content for the first time today, throwing himself through the wind and spray and sand. He quickened his pace.

Raoul had always been conscious of himself as if seen through the observing eyes of a second party, and even now he kept his body under deliberate control as he moved. Only once did he look back over his shoulder; the site of the swimmers was no more than a blot in the distance. In looking back, he paused momentarily, taking in the pastelled hues of the cliff, woods and sea. Standing out like a scratch in the bright paint of its background, the stone of Bleda Reformatory could be seen against the sky. Raoul jogged on.

The high ridge that marked this opposing end of the bay was closer now. Raoul could discern long grey folds in the face of the cliff and discolouring blotches of lichen. Stunted trees hung down like torn veils over sombre rock faces high above. Involuntarily he began to slow down. The shadow that reached out from this headland across the beach was as cold and colourless as gruel. He stopped, hands on hips, and stared ahead.

It was certainly possible to round this headland by way of a steep and stony beach which sighed beneath the burden of incoming waves. If the distant appearance of the beach that followed this one was a fair reflection of its nature, then the coastline was both lonely and beautiful, just right for such an afternoon run. But Raoul felt no inclination to cross the shallow mouth of the lagoon and proceed; his instinct turned his gaze inland, following the course of the river. After two minutes of scrutiny he once more took up his trot – this time along the bank of the lagoon, moving away from the sea.

It did not occur to him that the land here was by nature completely different from that at the other end of the bay. Geologists could possibly have offered some explanation for this in the thick and sterile white clay which lined the river, but no scientific analysis could have explained the gloom that lay over the area. Even the light that drooled down seemed tinged with a coarse and comfortless grey, an inverted reflection of the stagnant river surface. Raoul's feet slipped and sucked in the foul bog of the bank; on either side of him tall and brittle reeds stood quiet as smoke. All that was visible above their thin tips was the dark looming shoulder of a neighbouring hill. Raoul struggled on for some while until he began to shiver with cold. Only then did he halt and stand, arms wrapped around his chest, in the birdless quiet.

All at once the burden of this dead land seemed to fit over him like a lid onto a tureen. He was inexplicably uneasy. Pivoting slowly, he searched the dank walls of reed for signs of life. The stiff white blades of dry leaf stood close and naked as bone. He strained his ears, but the murky serpent of water beside him squeezed soundlessly past. Only the faint groanings of the surf were audible here – and barely so.

Raoul stood still now, ears attuned to the silence. He

worked his toes rhythmically to free them of the cloying mud. Absently he ran a finger up and down the nubbly planes of gooseflesh on his arms. He knew that he was truly alone.

But not happily so now – now that he had come so far for solitude. Raoul was of a harder solitary state, of the city. He had stood often at night in New Baytown and watched the harsh orbs of a crossroad robot, enjoying the gaudy gush of liquid light across his face. Often, too, he would take a purposeless ride on a bus through town, sitting quietly in the rush of bypassed visions, the constipated grunting of the engine, the tinny burp of the bell. These things rested in him; you could smell cement and glass in the air that surrounded him. And, because of this, he was uneasy now.

He heard the crackle of bent reeds long before the regular slosh of approaching feet became clearly audible. He froze, head up, trying to peer back downriver to determine the origin of the sound. He had an eerie feeling that something far from human was making its violent way towards him; the drab picture of river and reeds went a long way to supplement the sensation. But before long his darting eyes could see the clumsy figure of Spencer Hardy shambling up the bank. Raoul did not move in response.

Spencer almost walked into Raoul before he registered his presence. His head jerked up in surprise and he drew back. They stared at each other.

'There you are,' Spencer said.

Raoul nodded. It seemed pointless to reply. Spencer's face was the colour of old cheese in this light. Raoul studied the rims of his deep eye sockets and the cut of his smooth red hair. Freckles clustered dustily on his cheeks. His full lips were smiling.

'I saw you come up here,' Spencer said, 'so I followed you.'

'Why?' Raoul bent and worked a twig loose from the clay with his fingers. It crumbled in his grip and he shook the shreds off by snapping his wrist. Spencer was looking at him.

'I don't know,' Spencer shrugged. 'Just because.'

Raoul looked up at the sky with one eye closed. They stood

like that for some time. Spencer looked down and stirred the mud with his toe.

'So – how do you like it here?' he muttered at last.

Raoul broke from his reverie. He grabbed up a handful of clay and hurled it in a spray of white whorls across the river. 'How long you been here, screwball?' he asked.

'Me? I've been here … a year now.'

'Whafor?'

'Excuse me?'

'Whatcha here for, screwball?'

'Me? I'm…'

'Why d'you keep sayin' "me?" like that? 'Course *you*, screwball, there's no one else here.'

'Yes, you're right.' Spencer looked around. 'Maybe I'd better go.'

'I asked you whatcha here for, 'member?'

'Oh yes. I stole some things.'

'Me too. Whatcha steal?'

'Money.'

'That all? Christ, that's nothin'. You don't even know about stealin'.'

Spencer looked carefully back at him, hands on hips. 'I do, he said.

'No, y'don't.' Raoul slung a spatter of clay at him.

'Hey!' Spencer wiped at the blobs of white that clung to his chest.

'Hey yourself.' Raoul kicked another spurt up from the bank.

'Stop it.' Spencer's voice had a warning note.

'Stop it, stop it,' mocked Raoul.

Spencer grabbed him suddenly by the shoulders and swung him furiously. An oily fountain of turgid water rose and fell back; Raoul's head jumped up from the river, streaked with dirt.

'Hey!' Raoul exclaimed.

Even through streams of gritty scum, Raoul could see that Spencer was angry. It quivered through his torso and arms.

Raoul clambered from the river. He could smell its reek rising from him. The air was icy after the blood-warm blanket of the water and he shivered.

Now he was angry too, not at Spencer's reaction, but at his presence. Provocation, especially to anger, was one of Raoul's quiet, practical fascinations. People and their emotions were supple in his hands; because emotion controlled motion he found that he could guide events as he chose. He had expected violence from Spencer and he had received it.

But he had not demanded that Spencer be there.

He squatted on the bank to dry off, wrinkling his nostrils at the stench of disturbed mud. Directly opposite him, floating belly upward in the middle of the river, was the bloated body of a dead fish. He watched it move slowly downstream.

'Don't think you can just take over here,' Spencer said angrily. Raoul, ignoring him, continued to watch the fish floating away.

'Did you hear me?' Spencer spat.

Raoul stared unresponsively down the river.

'Did you hear me?'

The fish was no longer visible. It had slipped away into the misty recesses in the reeds.

'Listen,' Spencer said, 'don't be difficult.' He kicked angrily at the bank. 'I mean – I didn't come to look for trouble or anything. I just wanted to be friendly, that's all.'

'Why?' Raoul spun round quickly. His face was white and his lips trembled. 'I diddun wantcha to.'

'I just thought...'

'Well, don't. Just piss off.'

'Don't swear.'

Raoul stared up at him. A pulse jiggled the skin beneath his eye.

'We don't swear here,' Spencer said. 'It's ... ungentlemanly to swear.'

'Bullshit.'

Spencer hacked a thick wedge of mud from the bank with his heel. Neither spoke as it toppled slowly into the water. After some while Spencer opened his costume and urinated into the river. When he had finished he began to pace restlessly up and down.

'Why don't you just go away?' Raoul said. 'I don't wantcha here.'

Spencer stopped beside him, thumbs hooked into the waistband of his costume. He looked down for a long time, then sighed heavily.

'I just wanted to talk to you,' he said. Raoul stared obstinately away again. 'That's all,' he added.

'Go away,' Raoul muttered.

'You've got no hair on your chest,' Spencer observed, bending over and peering.

'Go away! 'Course I got hair,' Raoul said, pulling at the skin around his nipples. 'Here. Here it is. Y'can see.'

'That's not hair, that's fuzz.'

'It's hair, screwball. Can'tcha see? Anyhow, I'm only fifteen. Hair don't matter.'

Spencer straightened. 'You're not strong,' he said. 'You're thin. Look.' He pointed at the sharp outline of Raoul's ribs.

'I'm stronger'n I look, screwball. Stronger'n you.'

'Oh, no.'

'Oh, yes!'

'I'm strong.' Spencer flexed an arm and squeezed the bulging muscle appreciatively.

'That's not so strong,' Raoul said. He considered flexing his own meagre bicep, but decided against it.

Spencer studied him. 'We've got a group here,' he said.

'Who's got a group?'

'We have. I have.'

'Who's in it?'

'That's secret. Can't tell.' Spencer folded his arms.

'Oh, Christ,' Raoul exclaimed. 'How old are you?'

Spencer made no answer. They stared at each other.

Spencer began kicking at the mud again.

'What's it do? This group?'

'Nothing.'

'Nothin'?'

'No, but there are quite a few people in it.'

'What's it for, if y'do nothin'?' Raoul kicked at the water with an idle foot, looking over his shoulder at Spencer.

'Nothing. We just do nothing. But you have to be tough to get into the group.'

'I'm tough.'

'You're not.'

'I am!' Raoul looked indignantly at Spencer's chest. 'Y'reckon you're so well built, huh?'

'I am well built.' Spencer glanced down at his hard, flat belly and inhaled deeply. 'Anyway, that's not what I meant by tough.'

'Then what?'

'You've got to be able to take pain.'

'I can take pain,' Raoul said. 'I can take any pain.'

'Can you?' Spencer looked around. There was a long pause. 'There aren't any birds here,' he said.

'Not even seagulls,' Raoul said. He threw back his head and squinted up at the sky. 'Not a bloody seagull in sight,' he said.

'Don't swear!'

'Sorry.' He toyed with another twig that lay embedded in the bank. 'About this group...' he said.

'Hmm?'

'Can I join?'

'I told you – you've got to be able to take pain.'

'I *can* take pain. I tol' you I can.'

'Do you want to be tested?'

Raoul was about to answer when he registered the excitement that tightened Spencer's jaw and throat. Sweat glinted on his forehead, and his head was thrust forward on his shoulders. He could almost hear the frantic throbbing of the blood in Spencer's temples.

But equally sudden and compelling was the urge to take this chance to become one of them. Groups, closed circles, a hidden elite, were things that drew Raoul with irresistible force. He wanted, needed and craved membership of any congregation, nameless or otherwise, that drifted his way. Here even more so. Nothing could describe his terror of this place and its people. He desired their acceptance of him on any terms whatsoever. Even pain.

There was a long silence.

'I said do you want –' began Spencer.

'Yes. 'Course,' Raoul glared back at him.

Spencer delved into the money pocket of his costume and extracted a small red lighter. He held it ready and thumbed it into life. Raoul stared at the quivering yellow flame and shifted his eyes back up to Spencer's face. Only then did he understand what was required of him and his bones turned liquid.

Suddenly he had an overpowering feeling that the implications of this action were far vaster than the action itself. There was an entire world of meaning contained in his intention and in Spencer's excitement. The long drive down the coast towards the reformatory, the crippling constrictions of his apprehension, the events of the day and, more immediately, the sea, the sun, the sky, receded into the dim cave of trivia. This here and now struck his consciousness like a mortar. And yet … and yet he could not refuse now, could not call himself a coward, no matter what strange intuition decried this feverishly excited face that hung and shook like steam over his hand.

Raoul stretched out his arm with terrified slowness, seeing his own fingers trembling in rhythm with the jittering of his heart. The flame, slender and elegant as an icicle, lapped up around his palm. For a moment there was numbness. For another moment Raoul wondered with brilliant directness at the mystical connections that allowed this perfect feather of luminous gas to hurl such wavefronts of agony into the cramped confines of his skull. For one final moment his eyes were flooded with a tortured confusion of images that broke and fell through his whole body, images that seemed to leap at him from Spencer Hardy's hungering, unblinking eyes.

Then he wrenched back his hand, crying out, smelling the salty pungence of his own burned flesh. His palm was puckering before his eyes, the skin withered away from the moist redness below. He fell to his knees and plunged his hand into the river, crying out again at the scorching of the filthy water. Dizziness struck through him like a sheet of mist. Sounds fell from the air into his ears like stones. He heard the click of the lighter being put out, the soft slither of cloth as it slipped back into the pocket it had come from. He heard breathing too – loud, throaty breathing that rasped in the aftermath of pleasure.

'I don't think you're good enough to join,' Spencer said. 'Really not.'

'You bastard.' The words dripped from Raoul's mouth like the tears that silvered his eyes. 'You prick.'

There was a long pause. Then Spencer Hardy hooked his thumbs into the waistband of his costume once more. He sucked his teeth loudly and contemplatively. Slowly, with measured steps, he began to saunter back down the river-bank.

Raoul watched him go with an uninterrupted gaze, holding his hand pressed to his breast-bone. The ungainly figure shivered and dissolved among the reeds and soon even the sounds of its progress could not be heard. Still Raoul continued to stare. Still he held his burnt hand to his body.

And now somehow the moment shifted in time and overflowed its sequential position. It seemed to slide like water over the countless succession of instants that made up his life and taint them all. It trickled in bitter rivulets through the inside of his head and stung his mind more fiercely than the flame had his hand. Obscurely, it sculptured purpose from the coarse rock of his present situation, of his retention, of those he was to live with. Places and people settled like sediment in his brain. His purpose swam through the faces of Scott Berry and Joseph Hamilton to the solid central features of Spencer Hardy.

Raoul had often in his life been startled at the cold, reptilian shape of his own hatred and of the power he sensed in it. He was startled again now at its texture and force, and at the taste it pushed onto his tongue. His face was bloodless, his eyes fuming like hot tar above his cheeks. Currents of tension rippled through the muscles of his body, gliding up and down its length like sharks in a narrow tank.

Even now, reason shouldered up through the dank morass, advising speech with Scott, with Joe, with his *friends*. But the knowledge that he had come to this place for solitude, and would leave it in pain, was smothering. It choked such mundane things as reason. Shreds of unspoken anticipation drifted through his mental focus. He knew he would not mention his hand, would not speak to Scott, would not ... would not ... but stronger was the knowledge of what he *would* do.

He started walking back down the bank to where the white waves unfurled like banners across the bay.

'A day without comparisons,' Anthony Lord said, raised on his elbows. 'The sea is sky-blue, the sky is sea-blue, and the world turns.'

'Sorry?' Raoul asked, bewildered.

Scott, stretched on his stomach, picked up his head. The sun flayed his shoulders, buttering the dunes with blinding light.

'What are we going to do for ever?' he said.

'Live,' Raoul said.

'Exist.' Anthony scooped a wall of sand against his hip. He slipped his glance to Scott; sideways, momentary.

A shadow touched them. They turned to the west. Rising from the arc of the horizon, loamy gouts of cloud were twining into the upper air, swabbing the face of the sun.

'It will rain tonight,' Anthony said decisively, tracing a finger down the distantly swollen bellies of darkening white. Raoul closed one eye.

'How can you tell?' he demanded.

'It will rain tonight.'

For the first time Scott noticed a small and gnarled wooden jetty leading out into the bay about a hundred metres further down the beach. It exuded ruinous age, hirsute with bright fronds of weed. Wavelets blubbered softly about its supporting poles.

'What's that for?' he asked, sitting up.

'Nothing,' Anthony said. 'There are no boats.'

Scott stared at the contorted grey planks with growing uneasiness. There was something unnerving in dereliction, even if it was only the glimpse of past perfection and purpose one caught in it. He turned away. Anthony Lord was holding a book in his left hand, marking the place with his thumb.

'What are you reading?' Scott said.

Anthony turned the book over and studied the cover. 'It's called *In Defence Of Attila*.'

'The Hun?'

'I suppose.'

'What can you say in his defence?'

'I suppose ... that he was a victim of himself.'

'Sorry?' Raoul said again, frowning in concentration.

'But he was evil,' Scott cried. 'He killed men and he was evil.'

'How do you know?' Anthony said. 'Who are you to judge?'

Anthony's voice held a vehemence that drew silence down like blinds between them. Scott, trickling sand in meaningless patterns through his fingers, suffocated reply before it tainted the air.

There was a long quiet. Overhead, a dappled gull slewed across the slippery air and sank into distance over the water.

'He was just a man,' Anthony said and pushed himself erect, brushing sand from his legs. They stared after his retreating figure as he moved towards the pathway leading back to the reformatory.

'What's wrong with *him* now?' Raoul said.

But Scott was staring down at the twisted jetty that was a bridge between the land and the sea.

As evening muddied the clearness of the day the boys began to move in ones and twos back up the path to the reformatory. The bay became an inky well of shadows that surged up the faces of the cliffs, with occasional smears of crimson lying puddled in the warm stone. Tatters of sound fluttered down the shaft of air.

Raoul sat, hugging his knees to his chest, gently rocking, waiting until he was alone. Beneath him the sand cooled. At last all that could be heard was the stony spill and gargle of the sea. He rose.

Now the sky was almost completely flooded with oily whorls of cloud, hanging hugely like grapes over the land. He shivered in the first spits of wind. Still holding his arms across his chest, he broke into a run toward the path. For a moment, gazing into the murky facade of foliage that reared before him, it seemed that he would not find the way. Then, suddenly, the bare strip grinned whitely from the forest and he hastened up it.

The growing wind rattled the countless leaves about him with a harshness that seemed to fill all his senses. It could, however, only have been detected by one of the five – the sense of sight – (whatever the sixth afforded Raoul in his passing through the colourless world) for the others had lost their hold as trees and ground and leaves fell slowly away, becoming submerged in the soft brown putty of twilight.

It was only after they had showered and, with neatly combed hair, were tramping down to supper, that Scott and Raoul realized they had left their towels down on the beach. It seemed that they were the only ones to have done so.

'You'll have to go and tell Mr Bishop,' Anthony said. 'Usually we have to go back to fetch things if we forget them, but he might let you off tonight.'

Mr Bishop was standing at the entrance to the kitchens when they approached him. A fat black-haired man in his late forties, he had struck Scott as pleasant enough when he had met him earlier that day. He beamed at them. Raoul explained their predicament.

Mr Bishop plucked up a hairy wrist and squinted at his watch. 'Going to storm tonight,' he said. 'Better go down to fetch them now before you eat. Get wet otherwise.'

Raoul and Scott hesitated. The wind spluttered against the window-pane.

'Go on,' Mr Bishop insisted. 'Get a torch from the store cupboard in the entrance foyer. Only half an hour for eating, so hurry up. I'll watch your food for you.'

They left, subdued. In the great steamy hall, crowded with wooden tables, the rest of the boys seated themselves. Tureens were being passed from table to table, where masters supervised the dishing up. Conversation was flung about in the form of light bantering.

'Got burnt today, hey, Mark?'

'You're telling me. Did you see...'

'Sandbank out in the bay.'

'Yes, I saw a new boy sitting on it.'

'They've gone to fetch their towels now. Poor fellows left them on the beach – wouldn't fancy going out in this wind myself.'

'Reckon it's going to rain?'

'Boy, is it going to rain! Did you see the clouds –'

'Who is missing there?'

Startled faces.

'Sir, you said Scott Berry and Raoul Dean could go to –'

'Yes, that's two. I know about them.' Mr Bishop rose, crumpling his serviette in his lap. 'Who's missing from that third place?'

By now the whole room was silently staring, past Mr Bishop, at the empty place halfway down the table. A toothless gap in an exposed gum.

'I said – who's missing there?'

There was no reply from the innocently poised heads.

Raoul walked first, holding the torch, with Scott close behind him. The narrow white beam gouged a chaotic socket of sight from the darkness: swarms of leaves and vehement branches; the shapes of tree-trunks rooted motionless in the boiling air; even the wind seemed tangible in the watery clutch of that light. The path itself was easy to follow, shining like bone before their feet, but it was what lay beyond its fringe that Scott feared. Scared of the dark. Scared of the dark at fifteen years of age.

Yet, Scott, so much more to fear than simply no sight. One fears absolute vision far more than none at all.

The scene itself, clinical in its intention: two boys going down to the beach to fetch what they have left behind. There is a crushing normality in their hurried paces through the night, in the secure hand gripping the torch, extended, downcast. Yes, even in this simple fear of the darkness. But, lying deeper than the tread of their feet, deeper than the breaths they draw and exhale, as deep, perhaps, as the smooth plunge of cliff that snarls away to the left, is an awakened insanity. Somewhere, somehow, maybe as Raoul thumbed the cyclops stare of the torch into the night, or as Scott denounced Attila as evil by his actions, the awakening took place without the awareness of those who stood under its sway. For here, for now, the madness is begun.

As they stepped out onto the beach, they were shrapnelled with gusts of blowing foam. Scott, screwing up his eyes, saw that the knife crest of the nearest dune was frayed with tumbling clouds of sand. Pendants of spray laced the air.

'Where are the towels?' he shouted, the words splintering as they left his mouth.

'Here, here, come on.' Raoul was already struggling away, leaning into the slope of the beach. Scott followed, lowering his head against the stinging sand. They mounted the dune and gazed down on the next rise.

'Where? Where?' Scott cried.

'Where were we this afternoon?' In the glare of the upturned torch Raoul's face was carved of soap. Dark hair blew raggedly over his forehead.

'Where's the pier?' Scott shouted, his voice careening eerily away with the blown debris. 'We were close to the pier!'

Raoul flung the light in a ghostly mayonnaise blotch to the water's edge. The sea seemed black as tar, gleaming like slick and glossy fur. Scott ran down the passage of the beam, whipped from behind now, and stood just above the reach of the waves.

'Higher, to the right,' he ordered, and the torch darted away. Dimly he could see the ethereal outlines of the jetty hovering like a smudged chalk drawing just beyond the light.

'Okay, this way,' and they blundered off to the left. Raoul was swinging the torch as he moved, so that the sea flared suddenly out at Scott with every pace he took.

'Come down closer, Raoul,' he called, but there was no reply. For a chilling moment it seemed that he was alone on that beach; alone with a rushing mindless light that moved with soulless intent across the sand. He slowed uncertainly, feeling simultaneously foolish and fearful. When the light was past him, all that could be seen in the blackness were the neon stitches of the surf, off to his right.

'Come on, Scottie, here they are,' Raoul shouted back. Scott ran on a way, relieved now. And indeed, there they were, huddled like a pair of oil-sodden birds at Raoul's feet. Scott picked them up, avoiding Raoul's eyes, and wrung them out.

'Whatsa matter, Scottie?' Raoul said. 'What's wrong?'

'Nothing. Let's go back.' He turned away, holding the dripping towels at a distance from his body. Raoul guided him with the torch as they hurried back across the beach.

When they reached the high spur of land that, further out, tongued as the bluff into the bay, Scott recognized the concealed foreboding that had lain restlessly in his chest through the preceding ten minutes. They were not going to find the pathway.

Raoul stood at his side, whitewashing the choked forest

with light. He splashed the crystal beam into the forbidding mouths of shadow, thickly fanged with leaves. Nowhere was there the welcome glint of trodden sand running up beneath the trees. Behind them the wind rose to a shriek in the blackness.

'It's not here,' Raoul said, and there was an edge to his voice. 'The path isn't here.'

'Yes, it is,' Scott said faintly. 'It must be. Give me the torch.' He seized it and began to rip it back and forth across the undergrowth. Raoul saw fear in the trembling set to his mouth.

'Higher up,' Raoul suggested. 'Let's try higher up.' And he led the way along the edge of the forest, Scott behind him with the torch. The bank rose to their left, becoming devoid of vegetation.

'We're too far now,' Scott said. 'This is the cliff starting here.'

'Maybe there's another way up. Come on.'

'No! Not this way. Let's look some more. We haven't looked enough.' He stopped, holding the torch pointed down in a white pool about his feet.

'Don't stop, Scottie.' Raoul moved into the tunnel beneath the first of the trees that hemmed the cliff base.

'Don't leave me alone!' There was the scratchy sound of hysteria in Scott's cry as he bounded suddenly after Raoul. He bumped into him beneath the splayed branches of the trees, and they stood for a moment, breathing.

'Look, Scottie,' Raoul said, 'I only want to see if there's another way up here. That's all.'

Before Scott could reply, the sky was fragmented with a delta of blue flame. Raoul, looking back past Scott, saw the beach cut out in a hard gunmetal sheen, the water a pitted hide pegged out beyond it. He saw the images of roiling cloud transfixed momentarily, he saw the hanging leaves like corpse hands above, and he saw – thought he saw – something else.

Raoul's face in the torchlight turned grey as rain. He mouthed something.

'What is it, Raoul?' Scott said. 'What –

Raoul's reply was crushed in the horrendous and deafening crash of thunder which followed, rolling down the cliff like a boulder slide. Scott saw his arm outflung, pointing back down the beach.

'What?' Scott's voice was shrill. 'What is it?'

'Something there,' Raoul said thickly. 'Something following us up here.'

Scott jerked the torch up in a shuddering hand. The beam splattered like milk down the way they had come, etching long shadows through its course.

'Nothing there, Raoul,' Scott said slowly.

Raoul stared uncertainly, biting his lip and blinking. There *was* nothing … visible … and yet…

'Let's get out of here, Scottie,' he said. Ice was crusting his spine and his palms felt slick with sweat.

'Not up here, Raoul. We can't climb the cliff.'

'Not down there!' Raoul's voice was unnaturally high. 'I'm not going down there.'

'There's nothing there. You saw that.' Scott licked dry lips, staring at Raoul. 'Just a moving shadow or something. That's all.'

'Maybe. But I'm not going down there. Not until we've tried some other way first. Come on.' He turned and moved off into the close and treacly darkness.

Scott hesitated, his tongue like a dried pupa tamped to the roof of his mouth … and felt his feet, as though waterlogged, begin to tread deliberately after Raoul.

A cliff, two boys, and fear. There was nothing momentous in this slow progression through blindness, nothing far removed from what we have come to know in the everyday. Man has been seeking paths to mountaintops since his creation. Yet it would have seemed a pathetic quest, had it been observed by some being who neither loved nor despised life. There was something frail in the stabbing of light into dark. Through all the volumes of night, that single torchbeam was propped like a delicate silver splinter against the face of the

36

cliff. It barely seemed to move as they walked on and on against the rising wall.

'No, Raoul,' gasped Scott. 'There's no path here. We're too far now.' His breath snagged the raw edge of his throat as he paused, exhausted. Their way was clotted with tree-boles, knotted like distorted bars between the stars and the ground. Raoul took the torch from him.

'Let's go back, Raoul.'

'Hang on a minute.'

Scott watched the light drop low as Raoul crouched down, half-silhouetted against a furry white tapestry of under-growth.

'What are you doing?'

'There's a path here, I think. The ferns and stuff are all thin and trampled – the ground's wet here. What's this?' Raoul scrabbled through the sodden leaves, gripping the torch be-tween his upper arm and his side. Scott looked down and saw him pick up a shred of dark material from the torn soil. He held it up.

'This looks like a piece of someone's shirt,' he said. 'Check, there's a button on it.' There was a pause. 'It's wet,' he said. 'Look, it's stained with something. What's this from, Scottie? What's it doing here?'

'Starting to rain.'

'Huh?' Raoul cocked the torch up into the raging ceiling of leaves above them. Neither spoke for a time. Scott had his face turned up, waiting for another drop to fall. The wind snickered across the stony ribs of the cliff.

'I don't feel rain,' Raoul said.

'There was a drop on my face,' Scott said. 'Let's go back.'

'No, I –' Raoul jerked his voice back against his bared teeth.

'What's wrong?' Scott spun around, staring down the way they had come. 'What's there?'

Raoul bounced the light from the cliff to the scrub to the sky. 'There!' he cried hoarsely. 'It was there!'

'What? What was? Raoul!'

'I tell you, Scott, there's something here with us! It's close to us.' It sounded as though Raoul's vocal cords were burning. He was still kneeling on the ground, the torch cupped at a slant in his hands, impaling the earth before him with its beam.

Scott had no time to reply – did not know what to reply – and felt his throat turn into wet clay. The moment was trapped like a bubble in the stagnant river of time; an instant of horrific awareness; feeling his body poised in terror, their unprotected position under the cliff, the high emotion of his companion – and then a sudden cold liquid explosion across his clenched hands.

His cry was bitten deep into his chest as he recoiled, stepping back into a tree-trunk, staring upward into the branches.

'What, Scottie?' Raoul jumped up as he shouted out, leaping over to Scott. The cliff seemed to teeter threateningly over them.

'Noth...nothing.' Scott swallowed painfully. 'More rain, I think. That's all.'

Raoul swung the torch with nervous hands at Scott's face, and was about to pull it away from his shocked eyes, when he started and held it steady.

'What's that on your face?' he whispered. 'What's that there?'

'Where?'

'Between your eyes, running down.'

'That's rain. That's the drop I felt fall on me.'

Raoul stared, shaking his head, feeling his lungs shatter like glass against the top of his skull. 'That's not rain. That's ... that's...'

Scott wiped at the drop with an uncontrolled hand, then let it fall to his side again.

'God!' Raoul cried. 'God, God, God!'

'Where...?'

'What have you been touching, Scott?'

'Nothing, I sw–'

'Hold up your hands! Let me see your hands!'

Unwillingly, rusty with terror, Scott brought up his hands as though in supplication, hanging them like rags in the beam. For a nerveless and dreamlike second he gaped at them in disbelief. They were running, flowing, painted, with crimson blood; bathed in it from fingertip to wrist. He felt it trickling down a sleeve across his forearm. His own two hands – it couldn't be! – set in a rude bright wedge of colour – of red – against the grey background.

Then, spitting a soundless scream from his lips, he thrust them away from him as though they were not attached to his body, wrenching back spasmodically into the trunk of a standing tree. There was the incoherent grinding noise of bark, the shiver of disturbed branches overhead, a chatter of leaves – and finally, the slow and ponderous slide of something heavy above them.

For another moment there was nothing. Within and without the misty womb of white light that spewed from the torch – nothing.

And then everything.

With appalling and devastating suddenness, a gory, staring face of wide eyes and broken teeth slipped down silently into the light. Grinning hugely, it dangled upside down from the low grate of branches, swaying in front of them and trailing an arm like an obscene tentacle beneath it. As a belated heralding of its entrance, a confetti of fresh blood spilled down from the shaken leaves.

Raoul shrieked, the torch jumping like a wounded fish from his hands onto the ground. Scott had a momentary image of motion as the whirling beam sliced a wild arc from the world. And then there was only a deep, suffocating darkness. He heard noises without origin; high girlish screams, scuffles, and shifting stones. Raoul ... where was Raoul? He must be close by, because he was screaming ... no, no, no, no....

Scott realized with detached fuzziness that it was he himself who was casting out these incoherent tortured screams. With this knowledge, a sensation of sorts flamed into his limbs. He was kneeling on the ground with his head in his hands and above him he heard the dry rustle of that ... thing ... as it swung to and fro in the wind.

Terror. Terror so great that it doused all but the basic consciousness; flooded in a nauseating wave through Scott's body. He was aware of his own movement, stumbling on hands and knees across stones, crying, whimpering ('I tell you, Scott, there's something here with us! It's close to us'), his heart juddering like a pinned insect. Urine spurted hotly down his leg, puckering his pants against his flesh.

His groping hands found thorns and leaves. *Where was he?* Turning, he pushed himself to his unsteady feet and began to run. A heavy object grazed his shoulder and he staggered. *There's something here with me.* He fell drunkenly, still screaming, and rolled over.

Lightning neoned the coastline. In the grimy blurt of grey-blue light Scott saw the cliff on his left, and the terrible figure from the trees. Now, though, it seemed to be standing up, walking towards him, still grinning, holding out its limp white hand for his throat. Then darkness drenched them and he could no longer be sure.

Wetting his pants for a second time, he clawed himself up and hurled himself in the direction of the beach. Sharp rocks hacked at his feet but he blundered on, holding his arms about his face. He could no longer even scream. All sound seemed to be held in a molten pool at the base of his belly. Unseen things snatched at him, teasing, toying with his sanity. *Where was Raoul?*

He remembered Raoul's voice: 'Something there. Something following us up here.' God, what was he running into in the darkness? What was waiting for him here?

He halted abruptly, tasting fresh bitterness welling up in his mouth. His shoulders heaved uncontrollably; his hands fluttered against his chest. Then, quite distinctly, he heard the slap of bare feet on the ground behind him.

Moaning with fear, he ran on, holding his right hand against the cliff. *Something* was pursuing him; he could hear breath gurgling close behind. His legs felt gummed together and his head was seared with ribbons of black and white. All sound seemed magnified: the high burble of thunder broke about him like hail.

Suddenly appearing from the inkiness, the bright phosphorescent slashes of the surf glimmered palely in a wide scape before him. The sand beneath his feet turned fine and gritty, throwing his footfalls up at him like the savage gnashing of teeth. Was there a terrible echo coming from but a few feet behind?

The cliff to the right dropped away into the coarse density of foliage. He sprinted frantically across the first swollen dune, every fibre of his body tearing with effort. His flying feet struck a half-buried object in the sand and he found himself sprawling face down. Breath burst from his chest.

Lying stunned in the darkness, Scott began to retch. The acrid stench of his own vomit filled his nostrils, doubling his nausea. He arched again, emptying his stomach in a hot wave from his mouth. Pain bound his feet like barbed wire.

Where was the pathway? Where was Raoul?

Wind billowed across the beach, lifting fluid forms of sand high into the air. Scott heard the clatter of leaves and branches off to his right. Somewhere there was the path.

Feeling sand sticking in a rough fist to his groin and coating his hands like flour, he pushed himself up on his palms and crawled a few paces. A lucid image of that terrible, bleeding face blazed across his mind, and he felt weak. Sniffling, he rose to his feet. Once again lightning carved out the rise in front of him in velvet black against a virulent purple sky. Some cultivated civility in him still cried out against madness and he forced himself to stand still. His senses calmed with his breathing. He felt alone. He *was* alone.

From close by on the beach came the scrape of heavy feet.

He ran full tilt against the bank and was deep into the tangled heart of the forest before he tripped again. Pain sizzled through every part of him, spurting in sharp aches up his legs and arms. There was a cut across his right shoulder which stung fiercely. Holding onto branches overhead, Scott found his feet and stumbled on.

There was a violent crash off to his right. This time there was no question of mistake or imagination – something was there. Scott could hear the rasp of leaves and twigs beneath and about it, its ponderous movement. For another few seconds he hesitated: was this Raoul?

He could not wait to find out.

Dredging up his final reserves of energy and fear, he thrust himself, shrieking, into the waist-high surge of ferns and boulders that stood in his way. As he crashed out onto the hard smoothness of bared soil, he realized that he had found the pathway. Far ahead of him, hovering mockingly above the crest of the hill, the light that marked the tallest tower of Bleda Reformatory gazed lidlessly from the starless skies. Scott began to run towards it.

Distantly he heard a similar rending sound as ... that ... something ... fell out onto the path behind him. *Please, please, let it be Raoul:* the words ricocheted from temple to temple in his head.

Up, up the winding path. Sections of the way remained clearly imprinted in his mind: this familiar slope, ringed with boulders, lined with trees; these riven gullies crevicing the ground. Go carefully, carefully. This level stretch of sand that lies open on the right, open to a drop of two hundred feet...

Scott stopped, too scared to venture forward; scared that he might delicately move out beyond the lip of the cliff, might murmur, 'What? What?' as he turned over in the air, might still be taking steps on nothing as he plummeted into the tree-tops far below. He shivered silently, grinding his teeth to stop them chattering, clamping his hands between his trembling knees.

Footfalls beat up the path behind him.

Scott closed his eyes, bit his tongue, and sprinted ahead.

He only knew he was past the cliff when he ran into a tree-trunk on the far side. Finding the path with his fingers, he scrambled up it again, tearing at anything in his way, weeping as he ran. He could still hear something behind him, something pursuing him. How many creatures filled this night? How many creatures following him, seeking him, hanging above him?

In the blackness he ran into something. It was soft, it was alive. Hands seized his wrists in a hard grip. Beyond any further terror, Scott sank down and back. His body would not, could not, obey the summons of his brain: he was trapped. What was this that held him? Was it bloodied and grinning and toothless? His bladder was already empty, but he could feel it straining to vent again. Screams ripped painfully through his constricted chest, but found no passage to his lips. He felt dizzy.

'Scott Berry?' Mr Hall said, not relinquishing his hold on his wrists. 'Why have you been gone so long? Mr Bishop was getting worried about you.' Then he added sternly, 'Did you get the towels, boy?'

Falling into a calmness not unlike sleep, Scott thought dreamily: Homeliness. I have found homeliness. I am safe with homeliness.

But there was still an element of uneasiness, of uncertainty, of fear, permeating even this drowsy content, for Scott had seen, had recognized the recognizable in his own horror. The devastated, devastating, inverted face, the face that filled the deepest and darkest of Scott's nightmares, had been that of Joseph Hamilton.

Anthony Lord, as it transpired, was wrong: it did not rain that night. There were many, many faces gazing from windows through the dark hours, and many, many voices told the following day how the negro breasts of cloud had dragged pendulously away over the sea, and how the wind had slunk after them like a homeless dog. All agreed that it had been unearthly. One person was even heard to remark that it was almost as though the storm was withdrawing to await the right moment to break. Nobody, of course, paid any attention to that.

When the policemen and doctors, the newspapermen and ambulancemen, the concerned and the unconcerned, the living and dead, had all smoked off in featureless cars to featureless places, they left behind them less than seven hours of darkness before dawn, and the clinical coldness of their professional observations: Joseph Arthur Hamilton, aged fifteen, only child of Mr Gary Hamilton, aged forty-seven (and a widower), fell from a two hundred foot cliff at approximately 5.30 p.m. on the afternoon of the 19th of January, 1961. He struck an outcrop of stone 23 metres down on which he was instantly killed, his neck, right arm and collarbone were broken, and where he received the severe lacerations to his chest and arms that were the cause of the great abundance of blood found close to his body. Hamilton continued to fall and was caught in the branches of a tree below, where he also received a blow to the face which removed his front teeth. He remained suspended in the tree (his blood filling up the leaves around him) until he was discovered by two other boys at approximately 7p.m. on that same night.

If that same feelingless observation had noted the behaviour of Scott Berry that night, it would have seen that he stood, blanket-wrapped, at the dormitory window that viewed the sea. Or, more accurately, the night where the sea lay. Straining eyes could settle on no movement in the blustering darkness.

This blindness, to Scott, was no more than a physical extension of all inner nullity. One exists, while others cease. Intimations of immortality. Death. The taking and extinguishing; the ending and passing; the no longer and never; dust and ashes. Where was Joseph now?

Ironic, that those who live so gradually can die so suddenly. Falling, spinning through air, no more than an *object*; colliding with other objects; bursting, breaking, dying. That violent heart without motion. Limp. Gone.

Terror –

Running away from Raoul in the dark. No, Scott thought, it

was not fair that he should have had to fear. Not Scott. Not
he.

Joseph...

Joe had succumbed to gravity. To mindlessness. He had
been a victim of the earth.

Further terrible knowledge occurs: Joseph Hamilton, even
while he breathed, was never very much alive.

Where does one turn for comfort now?

Raising his eyes across the faces and voices, Scott met the
unfathomable gaze of Anthony Lord, who sat, cross-legged
and cross-armed, on his bed, above, below and beyond decency or corruption, friendliness or hostility. The permanence of that single figure in all the seething motion about him
was more comfort to Scott than a thousand consoling hands
could have been. For the first time in many hours, Scott Berry
smiled.

Later, when the building had finally turned to sleep as its last
resort for escape, Scott sat alone against the wall of the cloakroom. The fluorescent light gently bruised the tiled floor to a
faint shade of purple.

Scott thought he could never face darkness again. He still
held the blanket over his shoulders, tucking the fringes under
his feet. It seemed that even the heart of this building had
ceased to beat, in grotesque sympathy for all the dead things
of the world.

'Scottie?'

Scott stared as Raoul moved down into the room. They
watched each other timidly for a minute or two. Then Raoul
slumped down against the wall opposite Scott. Facing each
other across the cold tiles, they sat and breathed.

'So...' Raoul said.

'So...?' Scott said.

Again a pause.

'Do you think...' Raoul said.

'Do I think...?' Scott said.

A further wait.

'So do you think this place is good?' Raoul asked.

Another pause.

'Look…' Scott began.

'Look…?' Raoul said.

'It's not the fault of this place that Joseph is dead. It's not anyone's fault these things happen. He fell off the cliff. He'd been warned about it being dangerous. Jesus.' Scott began to cry softly.

'Don't swear,' Raoul said. 'We've got to be gentlemen here, you know.'

'Don't get bitter with me, you sod!'

There was another silence.

'Okay, look, Scottie … I'm sorry. I'm sorry.'

They sat without speaking for five endless minutes, while Scott controlled his sobbing. Raoul listened to the plop of his tears on the tiles.

'So what do you think?' Scott said at last.

'About?'

'About … you know.'

'Can't really think yet.'

'Yes, I know. I know.'

'It's … unexpected.'

'I know. I know.'

'It was a shock. Hey?'

'Yes, I know.'

'You got any smokes, Scottie?'

'Ahh, leave off with the smokes, huh, Raoul.'

'So now?' Raoul said.

'So now what?' Scott said.

'Do you remember … before we came here?'

'Yes. No! I – yes, I do.'

'The time Joe and us played baseball in the field behind your house.'

Scott was half surprised at the clarity of the recollection. Emblazoned across his eyes came a vivid picture of Joseph swinging the bat, light spearing its length in a silver fin; the sodden crack of connection; the ball soaring. And then Joseph, backed by high mounds of greenery, flinging down the bat as he began to run. The memory became slowed in Scott's mind. He saw Joe sprint, the air carving a furrow through his dark hair, dust hackling up behind his feet, the heavy sack of his belly jolting up and down as he moved...

'Yes, I remember,' Scott said.

'And the tree we climbed in the wood at the back of the field...'

Another crisp image: Joseph dangling from a high branch, kicking his legs and laughing. Scott, in a fork far below him, looking up at him. Between the shaking leaves, sunlight falling in liquid streaks that clearly defined Joe's form. Raoul shouting up from the ground, 'The branch, Fatso. You'll break that branch...' But they were all laughing, all of them...

'And the fight that Joe had with Giovanni "Minestrone"...'

Memory again – Joseph, face swelling and bloody on one side, head lowered, standing with tight fists. Looking up at 'Minestrone' with a half-mockery in his uprolled eyes, mouth opened, a rind of white teeth showing behind a split lip. And afterward ... Joe bending over a tap, lifting handfuls of water to his face, saying, 'Jesus, this hurts like Christ, ya know?' Not knowing that his face would one day be opened like a ripe bud on a sharp projecting branch below a cold drop of sky...

Images flooded his mind in a spontaneous rush. Fragments of an almost forgotten past. Joseph, wearing only his underwear, doing pushups on his bedroom floor; Joseph standing at a grimy urinal, shouting back at Raoul over his shoulder; Joseph lying in sleep on a slope of thick grass; Joseph, sitting on his bed, crying, as the body of his mother was carried away on a hospital stretcher.

'Yes, I remember,' Scott said. 'Yes, I do.'

They sat in silence, thinking back. Scott pulled the folds of the blanket even more securely about his feet. They remembered; they remembered. They did.

'Do you remember *this*, Scottie?' Raoul held out a coloured scrap on his palm.

Scott leaned forward in puzzlement, then hissed as he jerked back.

It was a torn piece of material, still stitched with a button.

'That's a piece of ... his ... shirt,' Scott said.

Raoul fingered the shred absently. It left his fingers stained the colour of mulberry juice.

'Scottie, what colour shirt was Joseph wearing?' Raoul said.

'White ... why?'

Raoul pinched the edge of the piece and squinted at it. 'That's what I thought,' he said. 'But...'

'But...?'

'This material is black,' he said.

'That's blood,' Scott mumbled weakly. 'That's blood on the material.'

'I know, Scottie. That's *his* blood.' They both stared at the shockingly bright little shred. 'But it's not *his* shirt. The material is black. You can see here.'

'Come on, man, Raoul. Ahh, come on, man.'

'What?'

'Well, what?'

Raoul did not look up. He stared at the button as though it were the glassy eye of a snake that held him mesmerised.

'I was the last one to come up from the beach this afternoon...' he began slowly.

'Bully for you.'

'...and I could see the path going up the hill from where I was sitting on the beach. I could see two people going up it.' He paused again. 'One of them was wearing a white shirt. He shouted back down at me, "You better hurry up here, shrimp, it's getting late." Do you know who that was, Scottie?'

'Joseph,' whispered Scott.

'And he was with someone,' said Raoul. 'He was with someone in a black shirt.'

'Who?'

'I don't know. They were too far away. I only knew the one was Joseph because of what he shouted back at me.'

'... I ... so ...?'

'Joseph went up the path with someone this afternoon. Joseph died this afternoon. Nobody saw him die ... so they say.'

'What do you mean, Raoul?' Scott shivered in his blanket. 'What do you mean?'

Raoul closed his hand over the button, then slid his eyes up to Scott's. 'He was pushed,' he said. 'Somebody pushed Joe off the cliff.'

The silence, this time, was crushing and chilly. Scott swallowed and shook his head.

'No,' he said, 'No. No...'

'Do you still think this place is good?' Raoul asked.

'No! ... Yes! He wasn't pushed, man, don't talk crap, how could he have been ... when ... look, I mean...'

'He was pushed,' Raoul said evenly. 'And as he fell, he grabbed at the shirt of the guy who pushed him. The guy who walked up the path with him this afternoon.'

'How do you know...?'

'I know,' Raoul said. 'Sometimes you just know things, right? I just *know*.'

'All right, knowall! So why didn't you tell the police that? Why didn't you give them the material and tell them all about it? Why didn't you let them find the guy who did it?'

Raoul dropped his eyes and gazed blankly at his curled fist – as though he could see that offensive piece of cloth through his fingers.

'Because,' he said slowly, 'we are going to find that person ourselves.'

Scott blinked numbly. 'And then...?' he said.

'And then we'll give him up to justice,' Raoul said. 'We'll hand him over to law and order.'

'But why us? Why couldn't the police do that? This doesn't make sense, Raoul ... it doesn't.'

'Just leave it like that, Scottie. I ... have my own reasons. Okay?'

'But why?'

'Okay?' Raoul insisted.

'You're mad,' Scott told him. 'You're crazy, Raoul.'

'Okay?'

'Yes, okay. Okay.'

They sat again without speaking. After some time, Scott rose.

'I'm going to bed,' he said.

'G'night.'

He hoisted the blanket more snugly about his shoulders and stepped into the doorway.

'Scottie?'

He stopped, not turning round.

'Yes?' he said.

'Spencer Hardy was wearing a black shirt this afternoon.'

'So were lots of people, Raoul.'

'Yes, but Spencer Hardy was wearing one.'

'If we catch somebody, Raoul, if we do – we will give him up to justice.'

'That's what I said, Scottie.'

'To law and order.'

'That's what I said.'

Scott felt very cold inside as he crawled into his bed.

Those hours that live around us for ever...

Scott Berry, enclosed in darkness from outside and within, found it sad that the sea should represent eternity. It seemed logical that the land, in juxtaposition, should be symbolic of all finite things. How ironic, Scott thought, that Joseph should have had to die on land.

Scott remembers: the first time he met Raoul.

The silent street, the sultry sky. Sunday afternoon. Scott is walking down the pavement, hands pocketed, head down. He is looking at the long shape of his shadow etched out before him across the cracked concrete, hearing his footfalls crack out in the humid air. He is, once more, alone.

Alone, but for sound. Scott becomes aware of a high whimpering that splits the belly of the afternoon like a blade. He looks up, and registers the pain in that crying. Pulling his hands from his pockets, he begins to run.

A narrow lane leads off to the left. It is brimming with golden light. In the middle of the road a dog lies on its side – a tiny beagle puppy. It is this animal that is whimpering in such pain. Scott can see its sides heaving. He runs down the lane and kneels beside the dog.

It has been hit by a car: the tyre marks are clear on the tar. Although the dog is outwardly unscarred from the accident, Scott sees that its chest is unnaturally distended, while its belly is strangely cramped. The strong and acid stench of fear permeates the air. The puppy licks feebly at his hand and watches him with trusting, terrified eyes.

Another figure crosses the road and kneels beside the dog. Scott and he stare at each other across the stricken animal.

'When did this happen?' Raoul Dean asks.

'I don't know – I just found it like this,' replies Scott Berry.

The dog begins to cry again; short bubbly breaths that shudder its whole frame. They both look down at it.

'What can we do for it?' Scott says desperately.

'Do?' says Raoul, surprised.

'To stop the pain.'

'Pain?'

'Let's call a vet.'

'Whafor?'

'To help the dog.' Scott stares at him.

'Whafor? It's gonna die.'

'But to help it.'

'To help it do what?' Raoul is genuinely bewildered.

Beneath their hands, the animal arches, groans, screams and – in a long frothy whistle of air – dies.

'See?' says Raoul.

Scott begins to cry for the paradox: that the sun still shines warm and golden on the bodies of dead puppies.

'Don't bawl,' Raoul says. 'We wasn't really allowed to keep it in the flat anyway.'

Scott stares at him again but the picture of his face is disjointed through a slow well of tears. This is how he best recalls Raoul: through teardrops.

'Why are you bawling?' Raoul says. 'I'm not, and it was our dog.'

Vapours, whiter than the salt that crusted the rocks down on the beach, began to rise from the earth and drift slowly across the ground. They were matched by the pale blister of sky that marked the moon. Elsewhere the night was calm and black. The disembodied chortle of the waves flowed as one with the mist; sinewy flannels of sound that twined between the trees and slid across the lawns. The only light that burned was that of the topmost tower. Even the cloakroom had become another cell in the dark honeycomb of night.

Raoul would never know what brought him so swiftly from sleep; whether it was the force of a physical touch, or the inexplicable sensitivity of the mind to scrutiny. All that he knew was that he was suddenly awake and aware, and that he was holding his body tense and stiff-armed beneath the sheets, as a small child might who fancies he hears a sound from under his bed.

Averting his head slightly, Raoul looked at the window on the other side of the dormitory. The tower light shed a feathery yellow glow outside that illuminated nothing. In its faint reflection he could just make out the beds closest to the wall. Relaxing, he shrugged back into his pillow and shut his eyes.

He had just settled into the easy rhythm of breathing which precedes sleep when he registered something foreign in the final image of the dormitory that he had taken in with his glance. There was no further mental identification than that:

something was simply out of place. Tensed once more, Raoul opened reluctant eyes.

His bed was ringed with quiet figures, standing without names or features in the gloom. Although there was no display of overt intent in their silence, Raoul sensed with a dizzy flood of alarm that they gave a definite charge to the air in the room. Almost, one could have said, an underplayed but wholly satisfied revelling in their anonymity. Shocked beyond challenge, Raoul struggled up onto his elbows.

But now the figures were in motion. There was the smooth melting of limbs through shadows. Even as he opened his mouth to protest, a rough hand cracked his jaw closed. Horror and incomprehension delayed his conscious registering of events. He was aware, only, of fingers compelling him from the sheets and up to his feet. Blood drained away from his brain and drew shimmers of white across his eyes. He staggered against flesh. A powerful blow to his chest threw him backwards. They stood on all sides.

An instant of clarity punctuated the farce: Raoul felt the coldness of the stone floor, the multiple grips that supported him, the steady ache of his chest where he had been struck. This awareness was once more revoked as he became submerged in a reversal of realities; fear and bewilderment became tangible, while the physical presence of those who stood about him assumed an abstract and detached nature, like gravity or death. He shook his head to clear it.

Hands lifted him from his feet, urging him forward in a guided rush between the beds. Nothing prevented him crying out but sound would not fall from his tongue. He made a soft whimpering in the back of his throat, but even his own ears heard nothing. Then he was put down on his feet again, pressured with an urgency of hurried bodies behind. Moving down the shallow step at the cloakroom door, he realized with an immediate giddiness that his lack of resistance was not wholly motivated by fear or even confusion, but in itself constituted a fascinated curiosity about the reason for this abduction.

Rough once more, the fingers spidered down his shirt buttons and his pyjama top was wrenched from him. Then the hands dropped, and, reacting for the first time, Raoul clutched at his pants. But his grip was prised effortlessly free and as he was hurled violently down onto the tiles Raoul felt his last protection stripped away with the tiny piece of cloth. He was, in every applicable sense of the word, naked.

Still he did not cry out.

Scott awoke the following morning amidst an unpleasant imbalance between past and present tense. The ghastly recollections of the previous night lay at odds with his drowsy relaxation in the early sunlight. Collecting the scattered pieces of his mind together, he yawned and sat up.

The dormitory was empty. Scott gazed down the twin rows of neatly made beds to the window. The sky was electric-blue and cloudless. The day would be fine.

Still intoxicated with sleep, he stood up, rubbing knuckles into his eyes. He stretched, spreading his fingers and groaning – then sat down again on the edge of the bed.

From the cloakroom came the sudden hiss of water. Scott lowered his hands and stared ahead of him with grim intensity, his senses momentarily transported through time. On the last occasion he had sat in this room and heard the shower, Joseph Hamilton had been with him. Strange, thought Scott, how the everyday makes the agony of our losses so acute. When we view the intricate panorama of man and his philosophy through general eyes, death does not lessen us as human beings. When we tread the familiar paths of routine, there is a space, something missing. A plump figure reclining on a bed. Gone.

Scott rose for the second time and shambled down to the cloakroom door. The fluorescent lights were on, tinting the woolly air with a pale glow. Somebody was showering. He could see a small figure moving behind the curtain.

'Raoul?' he called.

There was no immediate reply, but after a few seconds the curtain edge lifted and Raoul peered out. He looked at Scott with no indication of recognition.

'Raoul?' Scott said again.

The shower starved off into silence. Then the curtain was dragged fully aside and Raoul emerged, running with water. He did not look up as he began to dry himself. Scott frowned in puzzlement.

'What's wrong now?' he said. 'Raoul?'

'Nothin'.' Raoul glanced up as he rubbed the towel across his shoulders. 'Nothin's wrong.'

'Where's everyone?'

'School.'

'School?'

'Yes, *school*. Okay? Okay?'

'What's wrong with *you*? Something wrong with you?'

'Nothin'. I said nothin's wrong! Okay?'

Scott leaned against the wall, head tilted to one side. He detected an element of artificiality in his stance, but he could not define its cause. Then he recalled a similar pose from the previous day. He was standing as Anthony Lord stood. Hurriedly he straightened.

'The matron came up to tell us we don't have to go to school till later,' Raoul said. 'Mr Hall says so.'

'Why not?'

'How should *I* know?' he snapped. After a further half minute of quiet, he looked over at Scott. 'To recover,' he conceded. 'To recover from ... last night.'

'Where did *you* go to last night? In the dark, I mean. On the beach.'

'Whatcha mean, where'd I go? What's that s'posed to mean?'

'Don't get angry with –'

'Well, you – I'm not angry, screwball! Whatcha mean by that?'

'What's wrong with you?'

Raoul grabbed up his shirt in one hand and stalked past

Scott, looking straight ahead of him. Below them, the bell shrilled out. Scott ran his eyes over the cold walls, then he turned away and followed Raoul.

'Don't say nothin' to me,' Raoul muttered, lacing up his shoe on the window-sill. 'I don't wanta talk so much today.'

'Why not?'

"Cause I don't, that's why not. I'm not in the mood.'

Scott watched him closely. Light from the open window fell across him in golden tresses, robbing his downcast face of its flush. In the whiteness, his eyes seemed unnaturally black and deep. They did not blink.

'Hot today, hey?' Scott said.

'I said, don't say nothin'.'

'Just talking, Raoul, that's all.'

'Well, don't. I'm not in the *mood*, I said.'

'I'm also sad, Raoul,' Scott said with sudden vehemence. 'Don't think you're the only one who misses him.'

'Misses ... him? Misses who?' Raoul blinked. 'Oh, you mean Joe ... oh, yes.'

They stared at each other.

'Don't you...' Scott said in confusion. 'Well, isn't that why ... aren't you missing him?'

"Course I miss him.' Raoul glared. "Course I miss him! Don't think you're the only one, Scottie!'

'I don't!'

'Miss him?'

'No, no, I mean – I don't think I'm the only one.'

'He was a good guy.'

'Yes, of course he was! I didn't say –'

'My best buddy.'

'Yes ... he was. I know. I know.' Scott trod the water of bewilderment and tried to pinpoint his switch from attack to defence.

'I'll never find another buddy like that.'

'He ... yes, I know ... he ... he was a great fellow ... the ... one of the greatest guys I knew...' Scott's voice trailed off uncertainly.

He pressed his lips together and folded his arms, then moved past Raoul to the window and hoisted himself up onto the sill. The sea gaped away in a plain of heaving blue. As before, the sight made Scott feel slightly ill at ease. He slipped a tentative glance back at Raoul, who was putting something into his locker.

Scott had come to know the intensity of Raoul's moods and that aspect of their nature he respected. What he could not discover in his friend was the depth of feeling that necessitated such intensity; there was no evidence of it. Raoul was unmoved by beauty or cruelty or sorrow. His preoccupation, however strong, lay in the immediate. Scott knew that reason could never prompt compassion or sensitivity; such attributes were spontaneous. Yet Raoul appeared to follow clinical steps of logic to an emotional conclusion, a progression which Scott had never understood.

'What's wrong with you today?' Scott turned on the sill and faced Raoul squarely across the room. 'What is *wrong* with you?'

There was a pause. For the duration of this moment, which hung as fragile as glass above their heads, Scott stared at Raoul. A heavy, transparent mass seemed to blanket Raoul's figure. Scott could see his mouth working, his hands fluttering in restrained expression. They stood that way for ever. Then Raoul appeared to free himself from this overpowering weight.

'Nothin's wrong,' he said. He averted his stare and continued fumbling in his locker.

Scott looked away too, down from the high window. His face was set and hard. He had a strange sense of loss, of something gliding away beyond his reach. The delicate pillar of his past, a pillar that had relied on Raoul for its structure and form, was hidden behind a mist of inner feeling. Sadness squeezed at him. Sadness which rises when one knows that loss has come because of one's own shortcomings, one's mistakes, one's lies. Yes, lies.

Because he had lied. And known it as he spoke. Joseph

Hamilton had never been one of the greatest guys Scott knew, never more than an incidental figure in the landscape of fifteen years of life. But whenever Scott thought of Raoul, and felt the violent pressure of emotions that Raoul inevitably fired in him, always the plump shape of Joseph Hamilton would surge up in his brain. Scott was – had always been – aware of Raoul's affection for Joseph. He knew the pain his death had caused him. Scott sighed and settled his back squarely against the wall.

Scott remembers: going home with Raoul.

The body of a dead puppy dragged to the roadside. Standing. Waiting.

'Look,' Raoul says. 'Why dontcha come back to the flat with me?'

'Where do you stay?'

'Here.' He gestures to the building that looms over the street; grey concrete, filthy windows. Scott hesitates.

'What's your name?' Raoul says.

'Scott.'

'Scott who?'

'Scott Berry.'

'Berry? What a stupid name!'

'What's yours?'

'Raoul Dean.'

'Raoul Dee?'

'Dean. Raoul Dean.'

Scott follows Raoul across the street and through a doorway. There are stairs going up, dusty stairs, the colour of bile. The walls are patchy, with brick peeping through the plaster. Raoul goes first, trailing a hand along the bannister.

Raoul's flat is small and dirty. The windows look out over a parking lot. Scott is horrified at the state of the furniture; bare springs sprout like plants from the earthy coarseness of the chairs. It occurs to him that Raoul might be motherless: no trace of pride lies in the four rooms.

'I sleep here,' Raoul declares, bouncing on the sofa.

'In the lounge?' Scott says disbelievingly.

'Yes. Why not?'

Raoul is not motherless. Mrs Shirley Dean arrives while they are talking. She is a large woman with a wiry turban of red hair – not flaming red and bright, but dull and coppery, like old paint. She is smoking a cigarette.

'Who are you?' she says to Scott.

'I'm Scott Berry, Mrs Dean.'

'Mrs Dean. Listen to him.' She taps her cigarette over the carpet.

'Hugo's dead,' Raoul says.

'Hugo? Who the hell is Hugo?'

'The dog.'

'Oh, no! Goddamn it, Raoul, I said we can't keep a dog in the flat. How did he die?'

'Car.'

'I told you to keep him inside.'

'No, you didn't!'

'Well, you should've anyway. Dammit, you're eight years old.'

'Nine.'

'What?'

'I'm nine.'

'Don't be cheeky,' she says vaguely, and stubs out her cigarette on the wall.

'Can we get another dog?' Raoul asks.

'If Uncle George will give us another one. Where do you come from, anyway?' She directs this last question at Scott.

'We stay at number 17, Galego Lane.'

'Galego Lane – you must be rich. What does your old man do?'

'My father is a doctor, Mrs Dean.'

'A doctor. What's your name again?'

'Scott Berry.'

'Your father's Doctor Berry. Never heard of him. What are you doing here anyway?'

'Raoul invited me up.'

'I did not,' Raoul said. 'He just came, mom, I swear.'

'Don't shout at me, Raoul, I'm tired. I've told you I don't want your friends up here, pulling the place apart. Where's your father?'

'Don't know. Not here.'

'When he comes, tell him not to go into the bedroom. I want to sleep.'

'What about supper?'

'Just get it yourself. Goddamn it, you're eight years old.'

'Nine,' Raoul murmurs under his breath as she closes the door behind her.

From the dormitory window Scott could see minute figures leaping in the surf. The late afternoon sun poured down with the richness of ripe corn, striking from the distant carpet of pine trees a gauzy glow of colour. The shadow of the reformatory building lay long and pale across the lawns.

Scott was alone in the dormitory. He had chosen his site and time well. For him this window-sill was a platform that floated in another dimension. He loved its height; he loved the sensations it created in him. He felt as though the world lay stretched out beneath him in brilliant colours. The sill was a bridge between the earth and the sky.

His eye was drawn to another lonely figure. On the lawn a hunched shape cradled its head between its legs. Scott glanced down for brief seconds only before looking away. He felt the crawling and guilty uneasiness that accompanies the sighting of a cripple or beggar. The presence of the figure was so personal and yet so private that it could not bear scrutiny. So Scott looked away.

He knew his name but no more. William Lee. The night before, when all the others had crowded himself and Raoul, asking with avid interest about the events on the beach, William

Lee had slept quietly in his bed. During class, while Mr Bishop explained the intricacies of metalwork to an engrossed body of students, William Lee had slept quietly at his desk. In the afternoon, while boys swam in the sea and Scott sat on the window-sill, William Lee slept quietly on the grass. Sleep was his refuge and his life.

Anthony Lord slid like a cloud onto the window-sill opposite Scott. They smiled briefly at one another.

Anthony's face was new to Scott each time he viewed it; it was that sort of face. The sort of face which is forever surprising. It crashed into one's awareness with the force of a brick and the perfection of coral. It was sudden in its appearances, too, and swift. Over the last day Anthony Lord had glided through Scott's hours like a breeze.

Not since meeting Raoul Dean had Scott found a face so rich in mystery or so compelling in mood.

'Hi,' said Anthony.

The word, with all its connotations of the humdrum and mundane, fell emptily from his mouth. Scott looked past it at those eyes. There was more than flesh to *this* body. His very presence shimmered through him like light, in the slack arrangement of arms over knees, of clear blue eyes, of neat chestnut hair. Narrow and delicate nose, freckles, teeth ... all fell into the pleasing aspect of pattern. None of which went halfway to defining the hum that sizzled the air around him or Scott's understanding that he was the only one to hear it.

'Hi,' said Scott.

They sat without speaking, but it was not a stilted silence. Such quiet seemed as natural as breath to Anthony Lord; it enclosed him like a bubble.

'Why aren't you swimming?' Scott asked at last.

Anthony smiled again. 'Hate it.'

'You went down yesterday.'

'I went to talk to you.'

Scott felt a pleasurable warmth tighten his chest. His instinct pressured all his unspoken words, questions, comments, towards the inside of this tiny head before him; not in order to understand, but rather the converse. He wanted never to be able to comprehend Anthony's thoughts. His mind was as unfathomable as the sea.

'I've been watching you,' Anthony said. 'I get feelings ... you know? Feelings from things. I can hold a stone in my hand and cry. I watch the sky and I walk alone at night. I like to stand in the rain.'

'Um,' said Scott.

'I think I want you to be my friend,' said Anthony.

'Okay,' answered Scott. 'Why not?'

Anthony grinned, dimples starring his cheeks, stars dimpling his eyes.

They continued to sit in silence, now not looking at one another. Scott twined his fingers in his lap, looking down at his nails. His mind, always quick to scrabble for motive, considered that Anthony could be offering his companionship and words for now as some solace for the loss of Joseph. A temporary aid. Only time could tell for certain. He sensed more than this in what had occurred, however. Even if it were as simple as his suspicion insisted, he knew that the offering represented far more than a token gesture, an empty exchange of words. Anthony understood the implications of death, this death: the knowledge that so many moments had been and gone, but more important, that that number of moments cannot grow larger. That, as memory fails, it in fact grows smaller. Retrogression.

This and more, an even deeper understanding. In Anthony Lord's head. Identical thought to that which had run boisterously and strangely alone within the confines of Scott's comprehension; life being compounded of a countless succession of deaths. Living being to experience death. Not physical death always, but the quieter things too. Love. Peace. Indifference. Scott thought of Raoul and sighed. He added one to his mental list – friendship.

Down on the beach, lying on his belly on the steaming sand, Raoul mused over a grubby sheet of paper. His brows were hitched in concentration, his lips gripped between his front teeth. Behind his left ear rested a misshapen pencil stub.

He had been lying that way for some while now, while the pleasant sunlight melted down the individual components of his body into a relaxed and contented whole. He felt as liquid and energetic as custard.

His concentration, although apparently directed at the sheet of paper, was in actuality focused on a picture in his head. His lips twitched and pressed on mental words, as though trying to squeeze them into shape. The boys at play around him and in the water may as well have been spirits in another dimension.

At last he moved his hand. Slowly he tweezed the pencil from behind his ear and brought it down to the paper. As the lead came into contact with the sheet, he hesitated as though he had completed an electrical circuit; then, with furious passion, he began to write.

'Dear Scott,' wrote Raoul. He paused for a further second, then crossed out the prefix 'dear'. His hand darted again to a new line. 'I want you to help me. You must, please. Please, screwball.' He held the sheet at arm's length and frowned at it. Then he continued with reluctant slowness. 'Last night, after you went to sleep, they came and took me out of bed. They did things to me, Scottie, terrible things. Serious. Please help me. I can't tell you what they did. It's terrible. Really. They raped me, Scottie, I don't know who they were, it was too dark to see. It was lots of them, though. I'm so scared, Scottie, it hurts, I'm so scared. Serious.' A passing foot scuffled sand into Raoul's face and he swore. Wiping at his eye, he brought the pencil down again. Now his uncertainty became evident in his held breath. 'They're all bad here, I can feel it. You must help me. I'm scared. Mostly cause I can't stop them or anything. They've got a secret group here and they're all mad. Spencer Hardy's mad. I could kill him, Scottie, swear to God. They're bad people. I was thinking now, if you don't help me

– it's so easy to be bad. I could take over. Swear to God I could. When it hurts so much, it's easy to be bad. Serious.'

Raoul lifted his pencil and sighed. The afternoon was warm and heavy, pressing on him like sin. He raised his head suddenly and squinted through the heat. Up in the dormitory window, as though framed in the sky, he could see Scott and Anthony sitting together.

Raoul stared at them for a long long time. His face twitched. His mouth worked. He closed his eyes for a quick second. Then he crushed the piece of paper in one violent hand and dropped his forehead to the sand.

PART II

Existence does not, in itself, require measurement. To have existed is the absolute completion of being. Man, however – unreadable creature of night and day – demands a means of relating existence to the plane of existence. He does this by observing physical change and placing a stage of his own metamorphosis into parallel with what he sees in progress about him.

Scott would always associate a certain stage of his life with the tangled tawny splendour of the summer that enveloped Bleda Reformatory that year. The season had been burning its flame down the coast for the previous four months, but Scott had never seen in the grey interior of Raoul's flat the passing phases of the sun's heat. Here, at Bleda, it was very evident. The trees that lined the pathway down to the beach were kindled with warm colour, an interwoven patchwork of yellow and green and rusty brown that shocked up like smoke from the painted ground. Scott liked to walk through the forests, alone – or with Anthony Lord.

'A summer without comparisons,' Anthony said. 'Leaves are like flames; flames are like leaves, and the sun shines.'

Mr Eugene Hall made careful notes on the progress of the remaining two boys from the trio that had arrived at the beginning of the year. Scott Berry was coping remarkably well – he had many friends, enjoyed many pursuits and handled the manual aspects of his schoolwork better than his contemporaries. Raoul Dean, however, was a different case entirely. He had apparently taken the accidental death of Joseph Hamilton extremely badly. He was taciturn and uncommunicative, and would usually be found sitting by himself on the lawn in the afternoon. The only friend he seemed to have was Scott Berry himself. Mr Hall wondered.

'The boss wants to see you, Raoul,' Chris Murray said.
'The boss?'
'Mr Hall. He's waiting in his study.'
'Okay, I'm going.'
He went.
'Are you unhappy here, Raoul?' Mr Hall asked.
'No, why?'
'You seem to be ... withdrawn.'
'No.'
'Is there anything bothering you?'
'...No...'
'If you ever have a problem, please feel free to come and discuss it with me.'
'Okay. Can I go now?'
'Yes, you may go.'
Mr Hall wondered.

Scott remembers: meeting Joseph for the first time.

Scott and Raoul are sitting on the stairs outside Raoul's flat; Mrs Dean is sleeping and does not want to be disturbed.

A plump dark boy comes up the stairs towards them.

'Hey, Fatso,' Raoul says, 'where do you stay?'

'Number 204,' he replies.

'That's next door to us.'

'What number are you?'

'How long have you stayed here, Fatso?'

'Don't call me Fatso. I'm Joseph. What number are you?'

'Why are you so fat?'

'Why are you so short?'

After they have finished fighting, they go back to Joseph's flat to wipe the blood off their faces.

'Have a biscuit,' Mrs Hamilton says to Scott.

'No, thank you.'

'They're very good for you – I made them myself.'

'Well … all right. Thank you.'
'Why are you bleeding, Joseph?'
'Fight.'
'Don't drop blood on the carpet; it'll stain. Have a biscuit.'
'Can I have two?'
'Yes. Just stir the milk on the stove for a minute, please, Joseph. Barbara is crying.'
Barbara is Joe's sister.
'Barbara, what is the matter?' Mrs Hamilton says.
'He hit me.' Barbara says, pointing at Raoul.
'She tried to take my biscuit,' Raoul says.

One afternoon Scott stood on the edge of the cliff, looking down over the beach. Somehow this open brink seemed to embody the vital questions of his life; it had been the scene and cause of so much change.

'Gonna jump?' Raoul appeared at his side. Scott threw him an expressionless glance: that's not funny. But it was wasted; Raoul stared down at the treetops.

'What have you been doing?' Scott asked.

'Nothin'. Why?'

'I'm just asking, Raoul, that's all.'

'Well, I've been doin' nothin'. Watcha lookin' at?'

'Nothing.'

'You lookin' at where Joseph fell?'

'Raoul.' Scott said it tiredly, lifting his eyes to the spur of land on the far side of the beach.

'Is that watcha lookin' at?'

'No.'

'You ever wonder about that?'

'About what?'

'Joseph.'

'What do you mean, do I wonder about it?'

Raoul held out his hand. On his palm lay the scrap of dark material, with a single button.

'I thought you'd forgotten about that,' Scott said.

'Dontcha care, or what?' Raoul stuffed the material into his pocket. 'If they pushed me off here, would you just laugh?'

'Come on, Raoul, let's just –'

'You said you'd help me find … the guy who did it.'

'How, Raoul?' Scott turned to him. 'How do you expect me to do that?'

'Let's find somebody with a piece missing from his black shirt.'

'How will we "find" someone with a hole in his shirt? Obviously, if a guy pushed Joe he isn't going to wear –'

'Come with me now! There's nobody in the dormitory – we'll search the lockers.'

'You can't just –'

'We're only looking for a goddamn shirt, man! We're not stealing anything.'

'The lockers have got keys,' Scott said.

'Nobody locks the bloody things anyway, screwball! Remember – everybody's good here.'

'Don't mock me, Raoul!'

'Suit yourself, screwball. I'll do it myself.'

Scott stood motionless as Raoul walked off beneath the trees. His angry footsteps chewed the thickly-strewn leaves.

'Okay, I'll come. Wait!' Scott ran after Raoul through the flickering shadows.

After they had gone, Spencer Hardy rose from behind a nearby tree-trunk. Thoughtfully he stood at the lip of the cliff, flinging shreds of bark over the edge. They tumbled into the waiting branches. He thought they looked like tiny corpses in flight.

The dormitory was deserted when Scott and Raoul entered it. Scott stood at the doorway to keep watch, while Raoul moved down the room, opening the lockers and rifling through the clothes. He checked every black shirt, holding it up for Scott to see.

'Anyone coming?'

'Hurry, Raoul.' Scott was nervous.

'Okay, okay – I – wait. This one's locked.'

Scott looked down the room. Raoul was at the last locker against the wall. They stared at each other.

'This is Spencer Hardy's locker,' Raoul said stonily.

'Just leave it, Raoul –'

'The only goddamn locker that isn't open in the whole room...'

'Come on, man, Raoul –'

'Why do you think he locked it, Scott? Huh? Tell me why.'

'I don't know, Raoul –'

'I'll tell you! Because there's a shirt with a missing piece in it in here.'

'Ahh, come on, man, Raoul! Quickly, let's just go now.'

'What do you say now, Scottie?'

'Let's go.'

As they walked down the entrance stairs, Scott said grimly, 'If he pushed Joe off, he would throw that shirt away.'

'Why? He doesn't know we suspect. Anyway, where would he throw it? Somebody would find it.'

'Burn it, then.'

'With what? Nobody smokes here. You can't just go round starting fires when you feel like it, you know. I'm the only one with matches in the whole bloody joint.'

'Don't jump to conclusions, Raoul.'

'No, don't *you* jump to conclusions. I only want justice.'

'Then why not go and report Spencer Hardy if you're sure it's him?'

'I have my reasons.' Raoul smiled faintly. 'I have my reasons.' He walked on.

Evening. Scott and Anthony were sitting on the window-sill, hung between the fading gloss of sunset and the garish white lights inside the dormitory. It was that unhurried time of day when people move with aimless intent. Boys were showering, reading, talking. Many just lay on their beds and stared upwards. It was always an hour of quiet content.

This had become routine to Scott, this sitting on the sill opposite Anthony Lord. Although they seldom spoke, he felt as though they communicated countless feelings and impressions between them. He felt a charge in every movement of Anthony's. Their gaze moved often to the same objects, each silently registering what he saw and, in receiving, sharing.

Anthony glanced now toward William Lee, asleep, and Scott followed the direction of his eyes. He lay curled in a foetal position on his bed. There was an unearthly quality of stillness about his repose, suggestive of death. To look on him was like looking on an Egyptian mummy – a preservation of form when all that had once filled it had passed beyond recall. Scott shivered.

'He feels nothing,' Anthony said.

Scott looked back at Anthony and his thoughts flickered over the question of feeling. Better, he was certain, to be asleep and not have pain. Yet ... seeing the light of Anthony's blue eyes, he changed his mind abruptly. Anthony Lord walked the beach by night and drank starlight with his sight. He would rather suffer for the beauty of the stars than be asleep and safe. And this was better by far.

High-pitched barking sounded from below.

'There's that animal again!' Mark Archer said. 'I'll kill it one day.'

'You say that every time the thing barks,' Raoul said. 'Why dontcha do it, instead of jus' talking about it?'

'Do what?'

'Kill it.' Raoul moved over to the window and peered down into the gloomy twilight. Scott turned his head and stared down too. There was movement below.

In the last light the tall figure of a girl was discernible on the lawn, leading Mr Hall's spaniel on a chain. A niagra of thundercloud hair hung down onto her shoulders. Her gait was loose and flowing, as though her limbs were smoothly socketed and oiled. Raoul gripped the edge of the window to stare out.

Although her face was not visible to Scott from this height, there was something familiar in the way she held her head. A dim memory kicked at his temples and he too gazed unblinkingly at her as she moved. He knew that he had seen her before.

'Who's that?' Raoul breathed, leaning dangerously forward on the sill to observe her progress. His knuckles were white blobs of tension.

'That's Adelle,' Mark Archer said, coming up alongside him. 'Mr Hall's daughter.'

Scott recalled now with swift fullness a photograph he had seen on Mr Hall's desk the day they had arrived. A large black and white square of glossiness, depicting this girl leaning against a tree. The photograph had been taken at too great a distance to allow detail of her face to be clear, but her stance had been distinctive enough to remain in his mind. He watched as she vanished from sight below the eave.

Raoul turned about and faced the dormitory again. There was a peculiar trembling to his features that denied their composure. Scott eyed him uneasily. Further recollection swamped his brain. Hot nights of unfulfilled passion in New Baytown as he and Raoul sauntered on dark corners and watched the whores in their equally dark doorways. And once … a tall woman named Delilah, whom Raoul had met through friends at school. Scott remembered sitting in the front of a dirty station wagon while Raoul and Delilah thrashed out their sweaty tune on the back seat. He had opened the door and left them before his turn could come up, running down the street and away, sick and sad and sorry.

Scott watched Raoul move away, then looked back once more at Anthony. New warmth lit him; he grinned. Delilah and doorways and darkness fled his thoughts as Anthony grinned back.

'There's a madness on this place,' Anthony said. He was sitting on that high and motionless sill again, not looking at Scott, but out at the sky. So sudden and unexpected were the words that Scott started slightly. He had been studying the clean lines of Anthony's chin and cheeks with the detached interest one might focus on a fascinating rock formation or cloud.

'Madness?' said Scott.

There was no reply. The sun was sinking into the west with all the slow ease of an orange into mud. Light, watery though it was, still painted the landscape in drab watercolour.

Scott said again: 'Madness?'

'Can't you feel it?'

Unease stirred in Scott like a drowsy lizard on a rock. He couldn't help recalling Raoul's accusing tones asking, 'What is wrong with this joint?' Without answering Anthony, Scott turned his eyes into the dormitory. Spencer Hardy was arm-wrestling with Chris Murray; Raoul was sitting on a bed; Mark Archer was changing his shirt; boys were talking animatedly; William Lee was sleeping.

'Feel it?' Scott said at last.

'Since you came. There's something wrong here. Somewhere.'

Repetitions from the past: a swift image of a hanging face. Attila.

Scott expelled the terrible heave of disquiet that had boiled through his chest. He became aware that his fingers were painfully clenched on his knees. He relaxed them carefully.

'Nonsense,' he said.

He was somehow thankful that Anthony said nothing more. But in spite of his own tepid reassurance he became gradually conscious of what he had been wont to call normality. Bright shreds of memory fluttered past his open eyes; his senses meshed him in another time. Twilight. Home: the gun-metal pillows of cloud whorling in the fading sky; footsteps he could lay faces against; the stillness of the evening air like set and polished crystal; the last flame of sunset splintering the west. Cockatiels in their cage, drugged with night; feathered fragments of the twilight. Sleepy titters of sound from the cage. Mother. Denizen of the dining room. Anonymous. Her apron is the width and whiteness of her smile; her hair as neat

and dark as her displeasure. Father. Rejoicing in his swad-
dling clothes – the grey executive suit encasing an even greyer
executive. Glasses. Newspaper. The unacknowledged Clark
Kent of two worlds: the second has only three inhabitants.

'Nonsense,' Scott said again, uncertainly.

From far below the hysterical barking of Mr Hall's spaniel
came pulsing through the open window.

'One day, I swear...' Mark Archer began.

'...you'll kill that dog.' Raoul finished for him. 'We've
heard that before.'

Scott looked down. He could see the spaniel running across
the lawn, yapping furiously. As it rounded the corner, Anthony gripped his wrist.

Scott's initial reaction was to look at Anthony's hand.
Everything unspoken in the moment was communicated
through those long and slender fingers. Then he raised his
head and followed the direction of Anthony's eyes.

Mark Archer – silent, steady, strong – was leaving the room
with a quiet intent in his steps. Raoul sat staring after his de-
parture.

For brief seconds Scott could register no element of the un-
usual in what he saw, but suddenly the scene snapped into
context and he felt a quick wave of fear. Madness?

'Stop him,' he said. His voice was feeble and papery.

Anthony craned his head around the wall and peered
down. Mr Hall's spaniel was no longer visible, but its barking
came up in ragged bursts from close on hand. He released
Scott's wrist, but Scott could still feel the urgent pressure of
his fingers.

'Stop him,' he said again, more loudly. With the words,
conversation in the room petered off. A nameless expectancy
set every muscle in quivering stillness.

Scott would hold for ever the recollection of an open window, and Anthony Lord peering out.

He could not say for how long they sat in silence, while time
was measured only by the intervals between barks. Scott
looked out into the deepening dusk and smelt the salt on the

air. Perhaps they had been wrong; perhaps Mark Archer had gone out for a quick stroll before supper...

Below, the steady barking changed to snarls and bubbling growls, then cut off into a heavy silence that reflected their own. Scott dared not look at Anthony, nor at Raoul. His heart beat like an imprisoned dove against his rib-cage and there was a thick taste of metal on his tongue.

Stop him. The words were not even spoken this time, but burnt as if with branding irons across his forehead.

From much further away, at the fringe of the solid shawl of trees, came a high yelping and whining that terminated in a soft thud. That conclusive sound, although distant and barely noticeable, seemed to shake the very foundations of the building. Scott flung his eyes around and stared into those of Raoul Dean across the room.

'There is a madness on this place,' said Anthony slowly.

They did not see Mark Archer for some while – not, in fact, until they all filed in for supper. Raoul, however, saw Mr Hall's daughter Adelle come running up towards the reformatory across the lawn, bearing a dead spaniel in her arms. He thought that he had never seen anything so beautiful in distress: the flowing black ripples of her tangled hair, streaked with blood, were a shadow of furious autumn, and the deep molten pools of her eyes were silver moons of dropping tears. He stared, as before, for a long time after she had gone, as though she left the perfumes of her grief hanging thick and sweet on the air.

'I want your absolute attention, please,' Mr Hall said slowly. All across the room curious faces raised themselves from the plates to look at him. Scott glanced grimly at Mark Archer opposite him, but there was no acknowledgement of his gaze.

'This evening, barely an hour ago,' Mr Hall began, 'my dog was killed. Apart from the fact that he was as old as my daughter, and has stayed with me since I took over my position as principal of Bleda Reformatory, he was also a much loved pet and member of the family.'

Scott thought Mr Hall was going to weep. The headmaster's hands, folded neatly behind his back, suddenly fluttered loosely into view, like disturbed pigeons.

'From time to time I have commended you all on the fine manners and bearing that you have presented here. I have never had cause for complaint. Ever.' He stared at them, his gaze piercing. 'Today, however, brings me to matters of a more serious nature. Extremely serious. My dog –' He coughed. 'My dog was found at the base of the cliff. My daughter, who was walking on the beach at the time, saw somebody throw him off.'

There was a clammy silence. Plates chinked in the kitchen with the clarity of tuning forks.

'Somebody in this room,' Mr Hall said, 'threw my dog off that cliff. And I want that person to stand up. Now.'

Scott looked across the table at Mark Archer. The sudden clamp of shock he experienced was not entirely caused by the blank curiosity of Mark Archer's face as he listened to Mr Hall, but also by the fact that nobody else at their table was looking at Archer. Not even Anthony. Not even Raoul.

'I want him to stand up now,' Mr Hall intoned again.

'Stand up,' Scott hissed suddenly. Mark Archer glanced at him with raised eyebrows.

'Me?' he said.

'Stand up,' Scott growled. 'Stand!'

'What for?'

People were starting to turn their heads towards this sibilant exchange. Scott ignored them. 'Stand up,' he said again.

'What for?'

'You – did – it.'

'I did not! What are you trying to prove, Scott? Just leave me alone.'

'Stand up!'

Mark Archer turned away from Scott and settled his

studied concentration on Mr Hall. Scott's appeal spilt emptily across the floor.

'It is clear,' Mr Hall resumed, 'that the culprit is not brave enough to admit to his crime. So be it. But you should know about my feelings.' He paused to catch all attention once more. 'I am not happy with the general attitude that has raised itself over the past few months. Not at all happy. You are no longer gentlemen. I have heard frequent swearing. I have seen coarseness that I am not accustomed to. There is a slackness of will that worries me greatly. Very greatly.' He looked around. 'All of you know what I mean. I believe that this sort of attitude is what is responsible for what happened to my dog today. If the person responsible doesn't have the courage to stand up and admit his guilt, then we will have to attack the roots of the problem.' A further pause. 'Cut it out! Now!' His voice was sharp. 'I don't want any more of this! Since the death of Joseph Hamilton, something has been wrong with you boys. It is going to stop now. Now! Now!' Red veins made threads through the pale skin of his neck. 'I don't want any more of this,' he repeated, but his voice suddenly was much softer.

He left the room then, but Scott saw his eyes fall on Raoul Dean as, once again, he uttered those commanding, pleading words: 'I don't want any more of this.'

Scott turned up his face from the warm sand as footsteps thudded like an excited heart over the beach towards him. Squinting up into the sun, he saw Raoul bound over the intervening distance between them and crash down on his knees in the sand.

'I've spoken to her,' Raoul announced dramatically.

'To who?'

'Adelle. I've spoken to her.'

'Oh?' Scott raised himself on one elbow and rolled onto his side. 'When?'

'Now. Just now. I told you I would.'

'No, you didn't.'

'I did! Last week. After Mr Hall gave us that thing about how his dog was killed, and all. I told you I'd speak to her.'

'What did you say?'

Raoul looked out into the tumbling waves with narrowed eyes. 'She was sitting on a rock up there while I was coming down the path. I just went to her and said, "Hello. Dontcha wanta swim?"'

'Mmm?'

'She said her father don't let her swim when there's boys swimming.'

'Yes?'

'That's all.'

'That's all?'

'That's all I said to her, okay?'

'Nothing more?'

'No. Christ, man, Scott, I said no! Why d'you always have to –'

'Did you just walk off after that?'

'Yes! Anything wrong with that, screwball?'

'No, Raoul, I'm just asking you.'

After a long pause, Raoul began to run ropes of sand through his fingers. 'God, she's beautiful,' he said.

'Where is she now?' Scott asked.

'How must I know? Still sittin' on the goddamn rock, I s'pose.'

Scott pursed his lips. 'Don't swear so much,' he said. 'Mr Hall said –'

'I don't give a fuck for what Mr Hall said, okay?'

'Look, Raoul, I'm just –'

'Don't just, okay? You're always listening to his bloody speeches an' making like you care.'

'I do care. I do.'

'Listen, screwball, you couldn't give a shit!'

Scott shook his head in amazed exasperation. 'Will you ever let up on that?' he said. 'Will you ever –'

'I know he did it, screwball. I know he did it. These guys are crazy, man, I swear they are. You know Mark Archer threw that dog off the goddamn cliff –'

'Yes, I know. I know!' Scott sat up in sudden anger. 'And what must I do about it? Go and tell Mr Hall, when everyone else pretends it never happened?'

'Help me!' Raoul seized Scott's wrist. Scott remembered Anthony doing the same thing more than a week before, and he had the same sense of communicated sentiment. 'Help me prove it was Spencer Hardy who pushed Joe –'

'But how –'

'Let's break open his locker! That shirt is in there. That black shirt with the missing piece –'

'But even if he did push Joseph, he wouldn't keep the shirt –'

'He would! He has! I can feel it.' Raoul released Scott's wrist awkwardly. 'Let's break open his locker,' he said again.

'We can't just break into the guy's private –'

'Think about it,' Raoul said. 'Think about it.' He stood up and shook sand from his towel. 'Think about it,' he said for a third time as he walked away across the beach.

Scott remembers: bringing Raoul and Joseph to his home for the first time.

Raoul is struck into awed silence by the great white house and long trim garden. Joseph shuffles in the rear with his hands in his pockets.

'Jesus, you must be rich,' Raoul says. Joseph spits on the slate pathway and dabs at the saliva with his toe.

They play in the garden. The cockatiels thrill from their great cage beneath the tree. Mrs Berry brings a tray of cooldrinks and biscuits from the kitchen.

'Have a biscuit,' she invites Joseph.

'Can I have two?'

'May I have two,' she corrects him.

'If you want,' he says.

They climb in the trees that stand behind Scott's garden. There is a free air to the wild unhoused lot. Afterward they go up to Scott's bedroom. On the way Mrs Berry asks them where they have been.

'Climbin' trees,' Joseph tells her.

'Oh, isn't that dangerous?' she says. 'How high did you climb?'

'Fuckin' high,' Raoul says.

When they are up in Scott's room Raoul asks, 'You have your own bedroom?'

'Yes. Why?'

'Just askin'.'

'Do you want to play with my electric train?'

'Naah.'

'Let's play Monopoly.'

'What's that?'

Scott looks around in desperation. 'Do you want to play on my go-kart?'

'Naah.'

'What do you want to do?'

'Let's go climb trees,' Raoul says.

When Dr Berry comes home an hour later, they are sitting in the lounge drinking wine.

'He said we should,' Scott cries tearfully, pointing at Raoul.

'I didn't!' Raoul protests. 'Scott forced me to!'

Dr Berry sends Raoul and Joseph home and beats Scott with a belt. Later he goes up to his room.

'Listen to me, my boy,' he says. 'I'm not happy with the friends you brought home today. Your mother doesn't like them either.'

'Yes, but I like them,' Scott says.

'I don't care,' Dr Berry tells him. 'They don't – come from the – right side of town.'

'What do you mean?'

'Look, they're not nice people, Scott. Their parents are not

*nice people and their children will not be nice. It just works that
way.'*

'But why?'

'They're poor. That fat boy –'

'Joseph.'

*'Joseph. That Joseph's mother is very ill. I know, because
she's one of my patients. The other one –'*

'Raoul.'

'The other one's father doesn't have a job.'

'So?'

'They're not nice people. They influence you.'

'They don't.'

*'They do, Scott. I'm telling you. Why don't you play with
your other friends anymore?'*

'I don't want to.'

'Why not?'

'I like Raoul ... and Joe.'

'You'll forget them.'

'I like them.'

'You think you like them, but you don't really.'

'I do! I should know who the fuck I like!'

Dr Berry beats him for a second time.

'One day, I swear I'll burn this bloody place down,' Martin
Everitt vowed.

'So why dontcha?' Raoul said. 'Don't just talk about it. Do
it. Take my matches an' set the curtains on fire. One night.'

Scott, seated opposite Anthony once again, allowed his
gaze to venture beyond the sanctuary of the window-sill. The
darkness behind him seemed to surge past the pane with the
mindless force of the tide. He was conscious of it as he looked
at Raoul on his bed.

As he did so, the presence of that dark-haired boy rein-
forced itself with an almost tangible assertion on his senses.
He was aware – with the full electric awareness one has of
one's own being – of that tiny figure, its bones and skin and

blood. The concept of origin and, most especially, origin in dust, was a ludicrous one when faced with the devastating here and now of voice and eyes and smile. Scott saw Raoul sitting sideways on the bed, legs slung over the edge to the floor, hands in lap, face turned in unreadable profile. Yet – this was nothing, no centre of feeling, no nucleus of emotion and elicited response, without Scott's own presence to complement it. All that Raoul was was absolutely without existence without those things that existed in relation to him. Scott looked back at Anthony.

'Thirty rand,' Chris Murray gloated from the cloakroom doorway. 'I have thirty rand from my mother. I'm rich, boys, I'm rich!'

Scott tried to imitate the Buddha-like arrangement of legs that Anthony seemed to find so easy, and once again gave up. There was much about Anthony that Scott found difficult to emulate. They looked at each other carefully. A not unfamiliar sensation of frustrated curiosity stormed Scott's brain; all in all, he knew nothing about what went on inside Anthony Lord. Once only had he asked him what crime he had committed in order to be sent to Bleda, but the enigmatic reply had been, 'I am myself.' If Scott were to glance casually around the dormitory, histories jostled one another in his memory as he looked on each individual face. He knew that Martin Everitt had raped and thieved to earn his place in this castle of stone; that Chris Murray had fled his home and stolen money and food in a wild trail halfway across the country; that Spencer Hardy had assaulted an elderly gentleman and mugged a number of others; that William Lee was of unknown origin and had been found in a commune of gun-toting weed-smoking delinquents; that Craig Draper had been involved in the pushing of narcotics down the length of the coast. But if he looked at Anthony Lord, all he knew was that he was himself.

The mystery was prevalent not only in the past, but also in the present. Often he would come upon Anthony Lord weeping; not only flaw moved him, but perfection too. Once, when he and Scott had been standing on the beach, looking on the sun as it boiled in the clouds, Anthony had stood silently while tears ran like mercury down his cheeks.

'Let's make this a summer without sin,' Anthony said.

'Without sin?'

'Wouldn't that be great?'

'...Yes.' Scott stared at him. 'But why?'

'Why is obvious. How is more difficult.' He smiled. 'Wouldn't it be great if you only sinned when you were doing what you didn't want to do?'

Scott gave no answer; he had none to give. He understood the proposal, or thought he did; that transgression of moral bounds occurred only when acting in contravention of one's inner impulses. But sin was of necessity dependent on the concepts of good and evil, both of which were labels that characterized actions as passable or otherwise in the sight of God. Or any judge, for that matter. In the light of this, sin sprang from evil and thus from a negative and ungodly source. Scott remembered preachers from New Baytown, preachers with faces as dull and emotionless as the Sundays they lived for, speaking out against evil, advocating good, and threatening eternal damnation to those who did not follow this road. Scott remembered, too, the expression of pious approval with which his father had received such sermons.

A large black moth blundered clumsily across the outside of the pane and fluttered in through the slightly open window. Anthony reached out and caught it in the hollow of his hands. Scott saw with something akin to hurt this sudden and transitory picture: Anthony cupping the tiny soft bullet in two fearfully cautious hands. Then he pushed it out into the darkness and watched it feather away beyond sight.

'It would have been killed in here,' said Anthony.

As though with deeper vision overlaying his normal sight, Scott saw the goodness that was Anthony Lord.

'Hello, howsit,' said Raoul as he clambered up between them. Scott, unable for the moment to move his gaze from Anthony, saw Raoul's shape between them as a formless and obstructing shadow. Then he adjusted his eyes and took in the hard lines of the small dark face.

'Okay, then, don't answer me,' Raoul said.

'Hello, Raoul,' said Scott.

'See you guys,' said Anthony, and slipped from the ledge and away.

There was a sudden vacuum, an emptiness that cried out for voices or feeling to fill it. Scott and Raoul met each other's gaze and it came to Scott suddenly just how long it had been since he had sat this close to Raoul.

There was a burden weighing on their tongues, the heavy and immovable mass of countless past days that in retrospect were devoid of significance or meaning. They had been shared, no more than that. Scott, his mind rich with recollection of Anthony's eyes, knew that a lifetime shared did not necessarily constitute a lifetime of meaning. Moments gave years their meaning, moments shaped all time. One lived for moments of life, no more.

The space between them was suddenly filled with minute movement. A pale moth had pushed through the open window in pursuit of the unreachable light. Raoul lunged for it and gripped it in his hand. With careless fingers, he plucked the wings from its body. Holding it in his hand, he looked up at Scott and smiled. There was innocence in the smile, the delighted innocence of a child engaged in innocuous play. Scott stared back, paralysed. Then Raoul tossed the living wingless bud out into the darkness and watched it fall.

'Crash,' he said.

That same night Chris Murray's money was stolen. After supper, while most of the other boys sat around downstairs drinking coffee, he went upstairs to the dormitory. He remembered feeling that there was something ... somebody ... with him in the room, but he could see nothing. It was as he went into the cloakroom that the feeling became a certainty: he could hear the scuff of feet outside in the dormitory.

'Who's that?' he called.

The lights went out. For a moment Chris saw a flurry of silhouetted figures in the doorway to the cloakroom, and then heavy bodies seized him and began to beat him. Finally, when he was breathless and battered, lying dazed on the tiles, hands delved into his back pocket and removed his money. He was left as he lay.

Much later, he told Mr Hall that he had no idea who was responsible for the act. All lockers were searched without success.

Many nights later, thick cloud lay fretting and fuming over the land, pinning a stagnant waste of air below it. Scott tossed between sleep and wakefulness, oiled in sweat.

Finally he sighed up into limp consciousness. He lay, beckoning sleep, swathed in the throb of distant thunder from over the sea. Rude light spattered the inside of his eyelids: he thought it was the reflection of lightning overhead.

And yet it was too constant.

Scott opened his eyes, stirred by deep chords of memory and dread.

The curtains were blazing with high gouts of flame that whirled and knotted in yellow sheets up the wall. Lutulent black smoke roped through the room.

'Wake up,' Scott shrieked, stumbling from his bed. 'Get up! Quickly! Help! God! Fire!'

Figures moaned and turned through the dormitory. Eyes opened, startled.

'Fire! Help! Help! Fire!'

At last: boys standing and running and shouting.

'Fire! Help!'

Scott, simultaneously thoughtless and nerveless, ran at the fire, then ran back. His heart bounced like a tennis ball between his skull and his stomach. Through his brain ran threads of coherence: What do I do? What do I do?

A single unattached thought floated up between his ears in

white print: Raoul, this is your work. He dispelled it and forced logic into its place.

Fire!

Fire!

FIRE!

Scott darted back through the crowded doorway into the passage. People were running up the stairs. He glimpsed Mr Hall in his dressing gown. The fire-extinguisher! Where was the bloody fire-extinguisher? Scott ran his hands down the dim gloss of the walls. Not here! Not here! Other way!

Smoke had begun to ribbon out the doorway, above the heads of the frantic, fleeing boys. Scott broke through the desperate current and out the other side.

The fire-extinguisher was hanging, indifferent and insolent, on the wall. He clutched at it with shaking fingers, but it held fast. Cursing, he wrenched it backwards and sideways and, with a metallic snicker, it kicked free.

The doorway, at last, was nearly clear. Scott ran through it and into the dormitory. Flames petalled the far wall and gave crisp light to the disordered room. One bed was occupied. William Lee slept on, unknowing.

Coughing at the raw bite of smoke, Scott moved toward the blaze. His fingers fumbled ineffectually at the nozzle.

'Here,' Anthony said, appearing at his side. 'Let me help you.'

Five seconds later a thick gust of foam billowed at the ceiling. Scott aimed the narrow hose and began to sweep the flames in rhythmic circles. Heat caressed his face.

'Higher,' commanded Anthony. 'There, there, there – okay, move on.'

Slowly, the red light that painted the room grew weaker and weaker. When finally the hose sucked noisily at an empty cylinder, nothing was left but smouldering blackness. Scott dropped the extinguisher with a resounding clang and turned to Anthony.

'Thank you,' he said.

Mr Hall took form in the tureen of smoke. 'Who did this?'

he demanded. 'Who started this fire?' His voice was strangled and furious.

William Lee sat up in bed, rubbing his eyes and coughing.

'Is something wrong?' he said.

The window-sill, as it happened, could still be used as a conversation site by Scott and Anthony. The flames had done their main work on the wall above. For many weeks after the incident that section of the dormitory remained blackened and blistered, a scarred heritage of fear. The curtains, which had been fuel for the blaze, no longer existed.

'I want to know,' Mr Hall snapped, 'who was responsible for the fire.' He was standing at the doorway to the dormitory, addressing the boys. 'Come on! Who started that fire last night?' They stared back at him. He stepped into the room and paced down between the beds.

'Listen,' he said, 'fires don't start by themselves. Somebody here, whether accidentally or deliberately, started that fire. Was somebody playing with matches?' He looked around. 'Smoking?' No answer. 'Come on, I want to know. Now! Tell me!' Rage mottled the flesh of his cheeks and a cord flickered in his jaw. 'Tell me, damn you! Tell me what happened!'

There was a long silence while Mr Hall gathered himself. Then he walked up to the head of the room. 'Open your lockers.' he said. 'All of you! Open them up!'

They obeyed hastily. Mr Hall strode down the dormitory, rummaging through each locker he passed. At the window he turned, hands in pockets.

'All right,' he said. 'I haven't found the criminal. But I will. I will find him. I don't know who's responsible for what has been happening here over the past few months, but I will find that person. And he will be sorry.'

As Mr Hall walked from the room, Scott thought he saw his gaze fall on Raoul's neutral, empty face.

Next evening, as he raised his arms into the stinging cloud of water in the shower, Scott had a brief and compulsive thought: must I put others' lives above my own safety? As he answered himself, his hands lowered and crossed his chest, as though he placed a sacred and approving seal on his intent.

Scott twisted the shower into silence and slid through the plastic curtain with the swift fluidity of the steam that surrounded him. The dormitory was filled with talking boys, most of them awaiting their turn in the showers. Scott moved to the end of the row; to Raoul, bending over, wearing only his underpants, stuffing sweaty socks into a shoe. He placed a hand on Raoul's shoulder.

'Come,' he said.

Raoul's upturned face understood.

Spencer Hardy, lying in the farthest bath of the row, heard (as did the whole room, the building, the land) the wordless shriek of splitting metal from the adjoining dormitory. He was the first to grasp at movement.

Spencer Hardy leaped from the bath with clumsy haste and slipped on the puddled tiles of the floor. Naked, struggling, he floundered his ungainly way towards the door, as though battered from side to side by the erratic crashes of sound that still burst out from the next room. His protests were frail in the rush of solid blows that met them.

Behind Spencer Hardy, the doorway was thronged with amazed faces. Once again they were locked into stance for brief seconds, although not all movement in the room had ceased.

There was something bizarre – one could have said carnal – in the scene that confronted them there. Raoul Dean and Scott Berry, immersed in semi-darkness and in blind purpose, were hurling a metal locker from side to side across the room. Their near-nakedness, their glistening panting bodies – although countervailed by the clothed and passionless bulk of the locker – painted abditive undertones of sexuality into their movement: fornication of flesh and metal? As the watchers stared, the scene reached a climactic conclusion of sound. With a last shuddering squeal, the door of the locker skidded open, vomiting its linen innards across the floor.

Raoul stared down at them with an expression that suggested absolute confirmation of all suspicion. Scott, following his gaze, bent to the pile of clothing and extracted a black shirt. He held it up in the slab of light that tumbled through the open doorway. Then he flicked his eyes to those of Spencer Hardy.

'Tear your shirt, Spencer?' he asked.

'What are you doing to my locker?' Spencer Hardy manhandled his voice up from his chest. 'What ... do you think...?'

'Where did you tear that shirt?' Scott threw the garment down across the bed and took a step toward the group in the doorway.

'What shirt?' Spencer Hardy gabbled in his confusion. 'What shirt ... I...?'

'That black shirt.'

'I ... where?'

'Where did you tear it, Spencer? Tell me. Quickly.'

'That shirt ... was lost ... for a few days...'

'Where did you find it, then?'

'It just appeared back on my bed one afternoon. A couple of days ago. It was torn when it came back, I swear – I don't know how! It just went missing and came back torn.'

Raoul began to move towards him. 'Liar!' he said. 'You lie, you lie, you lie, you lie...'

'Wait!' called Scott. 'We can test his story.' He paused as Raoul turned. 'Get the piece of material,' he said.

'No,' Raoul said. 'No, no, there's no need for that.'

Scott was suddenly very still.

'Get it, Raoul,' he said.

'I – why? No ... look, I don't know where it is –'

Under Spencer Hardy's confused stare, Scott crossed over to Raoul's locker. He opened it and reached in. Then he walked back to the bed, holding the scrap of bloodied cloth, to which a button still clung with a small tangle of thread. He bent over the shirt and fitted the piece into the gap. Then he straightened.

'The piece doesn't fit the hole,' Scott said. 'It's a different shape.'

Raoul moved closer. 'The piece could have torn again,' he said. 'Maybe there are more scraps down there under the trees –'

'And the button's not the same,' Scott said. 'Spencer Hardy has different buttons on his shirt.'

'What's going on?' Spencer Hardy pleaded.

'So what –' Raoul began.

'So,' Scott continued, 'some nice person took Spencer's shirt and tore it, then brought it back. Obviously that somebody didn't take much notice about the shape of the piece of material, or about the buttons on the shirt.'

For a long, long time Scott stared at Raoul.

'Will someone please tell me what's going on here?' Spencer Hardy said.

Scott remembers: the first theft.

They – Scott, Raoul, Joe – are sitting on the grimy curb outside Raoul's flat. Ennui.

'Watcha wanna do?' Raoul says.

'Dunno,' say Scott and Joe.

'Watcha feel like doin'?' Raoul insists. 'Movies?'

'Too late. Started already.'

'What, then?'

'Play baseball?' Scott suggests.

'Naah.'

'Climb trees?'

'Naah, man, I'm bored with that stuff.'

'Let's go buy sweets,' Joe says.

'Got money?' Raoul enquires.

'Let's go get some from your mother,' Joe says.

'Sweets?'

'Money.'

'My mother's sleepin',' Raoul says.

'So whadda we do?'

'Let's...' Raoul eyes them conspiratorially. 'Let's take the sweets.'

Scott laughs nervously.

'From where?' Joseph says.

'Cafe.'

'How?' Joe is interested; he is watching Raoul, unblinking.

'Just stickem in your pocket when no one's watchin', an' walk out.'

'You can't do that,' Scott protests in horror.

'Why not?' Raoul demands.

'You'll get caught,' Scott says. 'They'll see you taking the sweets!'

'No, they won't.'

'They're watching for people who do that.' Scott is adamant.

'No, they're not.'

'How do you know?'

Raoul lifts a sly eyebrow. ''Cos I've done it before.'

'Stolen sweets?' Scott says. 'Have you?'

'Yes, of course. Lots of guys do it.'

'You'll go to jail!'

'No you won't, stupid – you're too young. Even if he catches you, what does he care about a few little old sweets?'

'But – they're – look, Raoul, it's stealing!'

'No, it's not. It's takin' sweets, is all. What else d'you wanna do now, anyhow?'

'Baseball,' Scott pleads shrilly.

'Naah, man.'

'Come on, let's do it,' Joseph says. 'Let's you an' me do it, Raoul, if he don't want to.'

'Okay – Joseph an' me'll do it. Okay?'

Scott sits miserably, hearing the sickening clout of his heart-beat ringing through his head.

'I'll come with you,' he says at last.

Inside the cafe they move between the high rows of goods. The sweets lie all about them like beds of bursting blooms.

'Fill your pockets,' Raoul commands, and they obey.

As they are strolling out the doorway, Joseph drops a box of peppermints; the sweets fly out like strewn dice.

'Stop!' says the shopkeeper.

'Run!' says Raoul.

When they have been caught, the owner locks them in a dirty back room, filled with old cardboard and straw.

'Shit,' says Raoul.

'I diddun mean to drop them,' Joseph says.

Scott starts to cry.

'Watcha bawlin' for now?' Raoul says. 'Nothin's gonna happen.'.

'We'll go to jail,' Scott sobs.

'We can't go to jail, man, we're too young. My father told me.'

'Your father doesn't have a job,' Scott says. 'My father told me.'

'So what?'

Scott has no reply to this.

'They'll call the police,' Scott says.

'They won't, man. What does he care about a few sweets?'

'He'll call the police.' Scott repeats.

'He won't.'

'He will.'

'He won't!'

The police arrive ten minutes later.

That night Dr Berry beats Scott as he has never beaten him before. Although the owner of the cafe has decided not to press charges, the name of Berry has been noted in police files, and Dr Berry knows that there are better means of spreading one's name. So he beats Scott, using the customary belt with an unaccustomed heaviness of hand. When his anger has expended itself, he gives himself to a maudlin regret and sits with his son for an hour or more. He tells him that he must never see Raoul or Joseph again.

'But why not?' Scott cries.
'They have a bad influence on you.'
'No, they haven't.'
'I certainly didn't teach you to steal.'
'We were bored! And it wasn't stealing.'
'What was it, then?'
'Just taking sweets.'
'You'll go to jail, Scott, if you ever do it again.'
'I won't – I'm too young.'
'Who told you that?'
'Raoul did.'
'He's influencing you.'
'He's not. And I like him!'
'I don't care –'
'I like him! I like him! I like –'
'I don't c –'
'I like him! And I don't give a fuck what you say!'
Dr Berry beats his son for a second time.

Scott and Anthony walked out one afternoon along the endless white ribbon of beach. The land was foreign to them here: high jumbled slopes lay about them, tufted with coarse greenery. Only the sea was the same.

'I'm going home this weekend,' Anthony said suddenly. They were standing, barefoot, in the bubbling white carpet of the shallows.

Scott said nothing for a moment, holding his hands linked behind his back. Many of the boys went home for weekend visits. A few were released on licence – such occurrences were not uncommon. Yet in all the time that he had been there, Scott knew that Anthony Lord had never gone home. He gazed out at the far horizon.

'First time?' he asked, still not looking at Anthony.

'I want you to come with me,' Anthony said.

Scott felt an unpleasant sense of being taken by surprise.

He had no time to analyse his own response, much less Anthony's motive.

'Why?' he said at last.

'That is, if you want to. It's far away – Johannesburg.'

He was absolutely beyond contact with Anthony's thoughts, adrift in his own bewilderment. Irrelevantly – desperately – he said, 'Johannesburg. Why so far away?'

'Used to be close by – Port St Johns.' Anthony flung a hissing handful of sand into the waves. 'My parents moved later, when they got divorced. I didn't want to be moved to another reformatory at that stage – so I stayed.' He looked at Scott. 'You don't have to come if you don't want to,' he said.

Scott was suddenly too aware, not only of Anthony's mind, but of his own. The landscape lay about them, sculptured in hard and sun-flayed stone, meeting the sea in the tatty golden hem of sand. When they were gone, this ground would remain as if they had not been there. It would tread their own presence and footsteps beneath its progress into time... Scott knew the enduring need to endure. In this small boy of crystal eyes and weeping soul lay a promise of permanence.

'Of course I will come with you,' Scott said. 'If Mr Hall says I may.'

'I see no reason why not,' Mr Hall said that evening, facing them across his desk. They were, all three, enfolded in the reassuring womb of homeliness that was Mr Hall's study. Although this image was still supplemented by the bookcases, carpets and warmth, a small negation did lie in the absence of the spaniel. Scott tried not to look beneath the desk.

'Tell me, Anthony,' Mr Hall said, 'you have said to me before that you didn't want the opportunity of being released on licence. Does that still stand?'

'Yes, sir.' Anthony made no more reply than that.

Mr Hall frowned slightly as he sat back. 'Is – your mother *expecting* you this weekend, Anthony?' he asked delicately.

'Yes, sir. She's coming down to fetch me.'

'And Scott?'

'I told her that he might be with me,' Anthony said.

'Well – that seems fine to me. I am prepared to let you off school on Friday, considering the distance you have to travel. Mr Hall glanced at Scott. 'We will talk about releasing you on licence soon,' he said.

Scott felt a meteor strike his forehead. The room rocked. Once again he was compelled to consider a prospect without warning; now, however, he recognized his inner reaction.

'I'm not interested in being released on licence, Mr Hall,' he said.

Eugene Hall stared. This lay out of the reach of his understanding.

'We'll talk again,' he said thickly.

As they left the study Scott ran his mind over his emotion. For a moment of imbalance, he himself could not understand why the thought of leaving Bleda Reformatory seemed so unattractive – no, even stronger – so horrific. Then he realized with a slow sadness in his chest – he could not hope to leave this place because that would mean leaving Anthony Lord with it. He could no more abandon Anthony to the past than he could see beyond the rim of the ocean about him.

They were coming up from supper, human scales in a moving snake that twined up the stairs into various dormitories. Scott was alone in the press of bodies, locked into his own impervious skull, moving by habit.

'Wait, Scottie!' Raoul's hand was urgent on Scott's shoulder, a meek dynamo of excitement.

Scott knew Raoul too well to contemplate argument or enquiry. He waited with him till the flow had passed them by. They were standing at a window that looked out over an inner courtyard. Below them brick glimmered in opaque planes.

'What –' began Scott, but he was cut short.

'Listen, I'm gonna see her tonight,' Raoul bubbled. 'Outside, down by the beach. Wanna come, Scott? Huh? Please?'

'Who –'

'Adelle, man. Mr Hall's daughter. I'm meetin' her tonight.

Wanna come?'

'How did –'

'She passed me in the corridor just before supper. I just spoke to her for a little while –'

'What did she say?'

'Who cares? Look here, screwball, if you don't wanna come...'

'Are you sure she's meeting you –'

''Course I'm sure! Watcha think?'

'When?'

'At half-past ten.'

'But that's after we've gone to bed!'

''Course, man. Watcha think her father'd say if I –'

'Yes, but how are we going to get out?' Scott raised his eyebrows.

'The window.' Raoul smiled indulgently. 'There's a roof an' a gutter. What more d'you want?'

Scott had momentary recall of this 'roof': a bare shingled chute, suicidally angled at nearly sixty degrees to the ground.

'Come with me, Scottie, come on, man! She's just beautiful, Scott – you've seen her, man, don't say no...'

Scott, despite his calm, was slightly and disturbingly surprised at Raoul's spontaneous display of emotion. He had not actually given consideration to refusal, but his resolution was spined by what he sensed in his companion. He looked for no warmth in Raoul, so that when he saw it, it was all the more openly received. One refuses the intellectual intent, the brutal purpose; but to deny the wistfulness of voice and heart, the distant places that shadow the eyes...?

'What do you need me there for?' Scott protested halfheartedly, but he allowed Raoul to catch scent of his weakened resistance.

'Support! Support! I need your support! You're coming, huh, Scottie? Are you?'

Scott tweaked amusement into his lips. 'Of course,' he said.

Lying in bed that night, listening to the drowsy shuffles and snorts that filled the surrounding darkness, he felt a small impatience with himself at having given in so easily. But he hushed his mind. If it meant the confirmation of humanity in humanity, any sacrifice became bearable. Even that of dignity.

Raoul came gliding over his dreams.

'Time, Scottie,' he said.

Reviving the sleepy awareness of his limbs, Scott sat up in bed.

He had left his clothes folded under the pillow and now he pulled them on with hurried hands.

From the open windows the roof beneath them seemed even smoother and steeper than his memory had pictured it to be. Scott paused for a moment, contemplating the open *nothing* that lay beyond that clinging white gutter. Die? Like Joseph? A victim of the earth?

'Go on,' said Raoul. 'Before someone wakes.'

As Scott swung reaching heels out over the sill, a wind kicked coldly across the roof. Crouching low in the dim light from the tower, he clung to the visible joints between those brittle-looking shingles. Raoul, no more than a blot of shadow, came dropping close beside him.

For a timeless time they sat there, shoulder to shoulder, gazing out beyond the sickly fuzz of light, over the hanging brink. There was no defined form in the darkness, only the pasty hint of objects or lines, defying position. Scott felt a deep foreboding.

'Come on,' Raoul whispered. 'Can't be late.' He scuffled his way across the roof, and Scott followed.

At the far side the wall fell away in a sheer drop. Thirty feet below, Mr Hall's study window gushed a pale beam out across the lawn.

'Gutter goes down here.' Raoul pointed at the bottom corner of the roof. He glanced at Scott. 'Okay?' he said.

Scott made no audible reply. His palms, although gummed over with sweat, felt as though they had been frozen into the unresisting tiles of the roof. The thought of bed, blankets and sleep was very inviting.

To Raoul, that beckoning darkness. Without looking back, he bumped his way down the roof to the corner, holding out warding hands to steady himself. Scott watched him go with his hollow belly forcing blades up into his chest.

'Come on, man, Scottie!' Raoul's voice slithered up the roof to him and he responded numbly. Skidding down in the wake of his companion, Scott felt a strange sense of detachment, of uninvolvement, in his own movement. He was an observer.

Then he was with Raoul, looking down the slim white shaft of the gutter.

Raoul went first, sliding down with agility, arms and legs working. When he had reached the ground, Scott followed slowly, metal rubbing its cold heat into his hands. It was only as his feet met earth for the first time that Scott became wholly conscious of how scared he had been. His body was giddy with fear and drenched with sweat. He shivered.

Now they were free in the open and altered scape of night. The sky was cobbled with thick cloud.

Drawing in the cool and bitter scents that entangled them, the two youths made their careful way across the lawns toward the margin of trees. There was no human movement to be seen.

Stepping at last into the beating pulse of the forest, Scott relaxed a little. They – he – could surely have no reason to be afraid in the rushing spill of air, the spitting leaves, the writhing boughs? They were alone.

They did not speak during the walk down the long tree-spattered slopes. The woods, though, clamoured with a multitude of hoarse voices. Stepping out onto the waiting beach, Scott forcibly repressed a recollection of a similar walk at night. He wished never to feel that again.

'Where is she, Raoul?' he said.

As he spoke, she came floating from the darkness, drifting her long black hair out behind her. Raoul turned to face her.

'*Two* of you?' she said, a little mockingly.

'No, no,' Raoul explained hastily. '*He* just came to help me down the roof. He'll wait here for us.'

Scott found no voice for his swift irritation. Raoul's glib replies excused, but did not answer. He felt very spare.

Watching them walk off hand in hand across the dunes, he could forgive Raoul. Seeing Adelle for the first time at close quarters, he had not found her beautiful; not even pretty. There was, though, an element of attraction in her self-assurance, in the obvious belief in her own infallible femininity. It was a facade, of course, but Raoul could not see beyond it. He had blinded himself in his longing. Scott smiled gently.

The belief in sexual infallibility was clearly not unilateral, Scott realized: Raoul pulled Adelle down to the sand within what he must have known to be visible distance. Scott sensed Raoul's unspoken pride, even from twenty feet away, a reflection of some civilized animality – the need to exhibit one's own prowess in the eyes of one's fellows. In spite of himself, Scott could not help watching.

And being aroused. Not by the limited scene enacted before him, but by what it represented: love devoid of lust. Ironic? When the wind came whirling past him in its fitful bursts, he fancied he could hear faint sighs, moans.

Raoul and Adelle were welded together by their lips, side by side, pressed against each other as though they willed deformity by pressure. Eager hands, clambering fiercely down each others' length, were pale blobs against that snapping billow of hair. Their clothing (a thin but immeasurable barrier), their restraint, their ... bugger it, purity – offset in Scott a sympathetic longing. Sacrilege ... he caught himself wishing a sight of naked limbs, discarded cloth.

He felt immediately guilty. There was no logical reason for this urge. He had no conscious need to see what lay beneath Adelle's dark and close-moulded jeans or her loose white blouse. Let it stay hidden. And perhaps Raoul had, after all, thought he and Adelle were beyond Scott's sight. He turned his back on them and stared at the sea.

Almost an hour later they came back down to him, still joined by their hands. Raoul was quiet and that same quietness filled his face. Scott, rising, dusting off his pants, knew full acknowledgement of his own motives.

'Are we going?' he asked them. They did not reply, but stood dumbly, washed about by the night. Scott smiled again and led them up the pathway, and then off at an angle to avoid the cliff.

As they neared the crest of the hill, Adelle stumbled and fell back with a cry. Both Scott and Raoul jumped to her side, but at the pull of their hands, she cried out. Scott explored her lifted feet. His fingers touched rough metal. He knew what it was.

A thick cord of barbed wire was bound about her ankles, biting into her legs. Her jeans had been torn along the inside.

'Who the hell leaves barbed wire lying around here?' Raoul stormed. He jerked at the wire and Adelle gasped.

'God, help me,' she panted.

It may have been the low sound of her breath. It may have been the silence that fell. Scott and Raoul simultaneously detected an arcane suggestion posed in their circumstances. Adelle had fallen on her back, her legs held open by the twisted wire, breasts jutting out against her blouse. She could not move.

Raoul looked over into Scott's face.

'Can you get free, Adelle?' he asked tonelessly, still looking at Scott.

'No,' she said. 'Please help me.' It did not seem that she was aware of what was taking place.

Raoul laid a hand on the inside of her leg, without looking down. 'Jeans torn?' he said.

This time Adelle made no reply. Her eyes glittered up at him like studs of ice. Raoul's hand had begun to move up and down the long tear, caressing the bare flesh beneath. Adelle gave a small experimental kick, cried out, and said, 'Stop that, Raoul.'

Scott was hypnotized with perverse fascination, feeling of no more significance than the boulders or moss that lay around them. Raoul's eyes had dropped at last to the staring helpless face below him. He lifted a hand to a breast.

'Let go,' she hissed and slapped out at his hand. Raoul, unblinking, moved his fingers up again to the row of inviting buttons winking seductively in the dim light.

When Adelle started to scream, Scott jumped involuntarily. Raoul paid no attention to her cries, but moved on with unhesitating purpose, sealed in the blindness, deafness, muteness, of his intent.

Scott became conscious that he was running away through the slatted shadows of the trees, fleeing in terror the high ringing shrieks that reeled in pleading pursuit. With the realization he stopped abruptly, gasping, then turned and began to stumble back along his path.

Adelle was lying as she had been, but was struggling to rise, the wire carving into her legs. It was only after his shocked eyes had seen her open blouse that Scott looked at Raoul. He was kneeling beside her, dragging open the front of his pants.

Dizzy now with horror, feeling the heave of blood in his temples, Scott rushed at Raoul and knocked him sidelong. His heart smacked his palate. Then he fell onto Adelle and, delirious in his frenzy, began to do up her blouse. He was bewildered to find her clawing at his face.

'Leave me alone,' she screamed. 'Leave me!'

'I'm trying to help you,' he protested, but she beat back at him. Falling back, he watched her finally tear free of the imprisoning wire. On lacerated, bleeding feet she hobbled up the dark slope, sobbing in her unremitting fear.

Scott, drenched once again in his own sweat, turned on all fours to face his companion. Raoul, still stunned on his side, gazed back at him with wild eyes.

'Why, Raoul?' Scott snarled. 'Why? Why?'

'It was only a joke,' Raoul said. 'Only a joke.'

'A joke,' repeated Scott numbly. He was walled in by unseen shadows. 'A joke. Ha ha.'

'It was all just a joke.' Raoul did not flinch as one final scream came rippling down the slope.

'Love,' Scott said. 'Love!'

He began to crawl away, knowing why he had been afraid earlier. This was a night of revelations. Adelle had freed herself from the wire, but for him there could be no escape.

Scott believed Mr Hall to have exposed his full anger to the boys on occasions past. He knew now that he had been wrong. When Eugene Hall summoned Raoul and Scott to his study at five minutes past midnight, he was mottled with fury.

Adelle was not in the room, but she had been. Lying in bed upstairs, Scott had listened to the muffled sound of her sobs coming up through the walls. They had sounded incongruous in their hysteria, almost an intangible contradiction of what Bleda Reformatory purported to represent. Scott, nevertheless, had shivered as he anticipated their consequence.

'You raped my daughter,' Mr Hall shouted, sitting low and livid behind his desk. Scott saw the soapy texture of his quivering hands.

'I didn't *rape* her,' Raoul said evenly.

'As good as! What am I to do with you? What *am* I to do with you?'

'I can't tell you your job.' Raoul looked down as Scott looked up.

Scott was speechless. Raoul's overt insolence lay beyond the fringes of normal reaction. Humanity in humanity?

'I will write to the Minister,' Mr Hall said in controlled tones. 'I will demand that your stay here be lengthened.'

'Thank you,' Raoul beamed.

Mr Hall clutched with slippery fingers at the desk top. 'I will have you transferred,' he said. 'I can have you sent to another reform school or a school of industries or a children's home...'

'Too hot to handle?' Raoul enquired. 'Givin' up?'

Mr Hall sat back in his chair and stared at Raoul. When he spoke again, his voice was unexpectedly clear and emotionless.

'Very well. You will stay here,' he said. 'You will finish your term. You will be gentlemen when you leave.'

Raoul said nothing.

'Wait a minute,' Scott said. 'I didn't do anything. I wasn't part of this –'

'You were there,' Raoul pointed out, amused.

'You were there,' Mr Hall repeated.

Scott blinked slowly. He swallowed all objection and relaxed.

'Wait outside,' Mr Hall directed Scott.

Standing in the passage, Scott heard six vicious cracks rip out from behind the closed door. Minutes later, Raoul emerged, a little paler than before. Wordlessly, he motioned Scott through the door.

Mr Hall held his cane in restless hands, but he was seated at his desk.

'Come in, shut the door,' he said. 'Sit down. I want to talk to you.'

Scott obeyed, all feeling inside him dead.

'I will send Adelle away to her mother,' Mr Hall said. He looked at Scott. 'Tell me what happened.'

Scott told him everything.

'First my dog, then my building, now my daughter,' Mr Hall said. 'What comes next?'

'The people,' Scott said.

'It has all happened since you and Raoul Dean and Joseph Hamilton came here.' Mr Hall pursed his lips. 'And yet I can't believe that you are responsible. He – yes,' he pointed at the door, and beyond, 'but not you, Scott.'

'I'm not,' Scott said. 'It's not me. It's Raoul.'

'If I make a report on him to the Minister,' Mr Hall said, 'the Minister can order that he be moved to an observation centre. In another six months he will either return, be transferred – or discharged.'

'Does that solve anything?' Scott asked. 'If he returns – it will be the same thing. If he is transferred, the problem only becomes that of someone else. If he is discharged, the problem becomes that of society.'

'Society,' Mr Hall murmured. 'We had our own here, in the

reformatory. We had order and discipline. Till all this start-ed.' He arched the cane in his hands. 'We – I – have never had to resort to external help before. Bleda Reformatory had no need of assistance from others.' He paused. 'Even if I report him to the Minister, the only proof I have is what happened tonight. I have no evidence about – anything else. But I know. I know.'

They sat silently, staring at each other.

Scott remembers: the second theft.

They – Scott, Raoul, Joe – are walking down the row of shops in Governor Street. They pass a jeweller's store.

'Just get a load of that thing.' Raoul points at a gaudy neck-lace of fluted pearl and coloured stone. 'My mother would love that.'

'You can't afford it, Raoul,' Scott says. The price tag smirks up at them.

Raoul winks and they walk on. Five metres down the road he stops and looks back. 'I can't afford to buy it,' he says.

'No,' Joseph agrees.

'Just wait a second,' Scott cries out in alarm. 'We've been caught before!'

'And nothin' happened, hey? So watcha worried about?'

'They'll send us –'

'To jail?' Raoul finishes the sentence mockingly. 'I told you, Scottie, we're too young.'

'It's wrong to steal,' Scott cries desperately.

'Wrong? What's wrong an' what's right? You're just sayin' that because your father told you.'

Scott feels a deep twinge: the accusation is true. He thinks then of his father and his father's world; the warmth and light and white plaster and bird cages. He thinks of Raoul's battered couch, the neatly folded blanket on the floor beneath. He real-izes that human bonds override circumstance and pride; they, in fact, create them.

That night, the three boys come sauntering down the poorly lit street. Raoul, in compliance with the convention demanded by countless gangster movies and novels, has a brick, wrapped in newspaper, firmly gripped in his coat pocket.

They stand for a while, awaiting their moment. Then Raoul removes the brick, and with a single swift swipe, hurls it through the window. The noise of shattering glass is immense in the unsuspecting evening. It is immediately followed by an alarm bell in the shop.

Raoul cuts himself while fumbling through the broken debris for his prize. When he finally grasps it with bleeding hands, the trio sprints down the pavement and around the corner into –

Two policemen. This time it seems that no interlude is provided for remorse between the act and its result, uniformed in that familiar stiff blue.

They are taken to the police-station and locked up while the jeweller is contacted, together with their respective parents. Raoul's mother is upset at having been woken.

The jeweller decides to press charges.

Raoul, Joe and Scott are allowed to return to their homes, but must appear in a children's court at ten-thirty the following Monday. They are placed in the official custody of their parents.

Dr Berry beats Scott severely that night. Afterward, Scott lies crying in his bed, wishing for sleep that he knows will not come.

Suddenly there is a faint tinkle of pebbles against his window. Knowing what he will see outside, Scott rises and goes over.

Moonlight enamels the silent garden. Raoul and Joe are standing below, gazing up at him.

Scott swiftly puts on his clothes and lets himself out of the house to join them. Quieter than the settling dew, they move away from home and harm.

With the dawn, they find themselves in a landscape they have never seen before. Horizons beckon them on.

Three days before Scott was to visit Anthony Lord at home, Chris Murray and Martin Everitt left the reformatory. To call it an escape would hardly have been accurate, for there were no measures to prevent their leaving. With the morning came the discovery of two empty beds and a new spirit of conscious uneasiness through the entire building.

The two, it later transpired, had made their way along the beach. They managed to run for more than twenty kilometres before the police alert seized them in its seeking jaws.

More disturbing than the concept of attempted escape was the momentary glimpse that Scott had of Chris and Martin as they waited outside Mr Hall's study. The harrowed haunted faces seemed to epitomize his own unquenchable fear. They had run from what was hunting him down too.

They were removed soon after by their apprehender (a local policeman) to a 'place of safety', the locality of which was unknown to the remaining boys. As neither of them were older than eighteen years of age, they had, in escaping, committed no legal offence. They were, nevertheless, taken to appear before a commissioner of child welfare of the immediate district. Although the reformatory was never to house them again, the consequences of their deed enveloped the lives of those they had left behind.

A special enquiry on Bleda Reformatory was authorized for two weeks' time. The building waited expectantly.

The next day the unblemished sky was burning with light and most of the boys went down to the beach. Lying on the warm sand, Scott and Anthony talked quietly.

As the sun began its final glide down to the water, one of the boys discovered a soft and impressionable surface peeping through the foliage on the rising cliff face. By scratching at it with a pointed twig, he carved out his name in clear letters. This initiated a general exodus to the cliff, with every boy intent on cutting his name into the cool soil.

'Shall we?' asked Anthony, as more figures came hurrying eagerly past them.

Scott folded an arm over his eyes. 'You go,' he said. 'I'll come along later.'

Anthony rose and left him.

Much later, as shadows began to unroll from the cliffs, Scott pushed himself up and walked to the open face of sand. Nobody was standing there now, but their names gazed silently back at him. He bent and picked up a discarded twig, looking all the time for where Anthony had left his mark.

He could not see it at first. The names crawled motionlessly before him: Daryn Peters, Kevin Krummeck, Graham Poole, Owen Fair ... but no Anthony Lord. No Anthony Lord.

At the far side of the surface he found Anthony's mark.

Amid the elaborate script, the loops and tails and lines, one word was inscribed in neat print: 'AGONY'. From the soil, this statement glimmered in the fading light. Agony. Anthony Lord had left behind his legacy.

Scott dropped the twig and began to walk slowly back across the beach.

That evening, William Lee ceased to be unknowing.

They – the whole dormitory – were settling into bed, nobody speaking. Silent because of fear, perhaps: fear of what they might awaken to – the burning wall, the far-off crying.

When the first terrible shriek gashed the quiet, Scott had a swift memory of Adelle's uplifted face. He suffered the instinctive conviction that the cry originated inside his own head. Turning, though, his ribs enclosing a barrel of ice, he saw the entire room moving in this selfsame dread of what they might find.

William Lee seemed still to be in the depths of his own reality – sleep. Yet even as they stepped towards him with reluctant feet, his next scream broke the outer mask of repose. With wide, bulging eyes and frothing mouth, he flung himself to the floor and curled up into a violent ball. The unending, quivering shrieks hammered their way from his chest.

'Help him,' cried Scott. 'God, help him, somebody!'

The reaching hands of his fellows touched William Lee in a desperate attempt at consolation. But he lashed out, still screaming with shrill ferocity. Coherence dragged out words from the sound.

'Leave me, leave me, leave me!'

'Shut him up!' snarled Raoul. 'Make him keep quiet!'

The room fell silent. William Lee whimpered. Raoul crossed over to him in two steps and kicked at his exposed back. With the heavy thud of expelled breath, Scott moved forward.

'Stop, Raoul, stop that! Stop! Stop!'

William Lee began to scream again.

When they finally took him away to the clinic, he had been sedated and silenced; he was sleeping once again.

'Hysteria,' said the doctor.

For Scott Berry, left behind once more, there remained only a vision of that nodding head as it swayed its way into the protection of dreams, and the distant echoes of ululations that had cried out against the dark.

Attila. Attila.

During that same night, Scott woke. The room was hazy with pleated thongs of moonlight, blue and smoky as the sea. He eased himself round to a fresh position, nudging his shoulder more comfortably into the mattress. His open eyes were on the rows of beds, but it took his sleep-numbed mind five seconds to register what it was seeing.

The room was filled with silent figures, converging with quiet assurance on Raoul's bed. The dim shadow that stained the air robbed their features of definition and identity, though the target of their movement was certainly clear. If Scott had concentrated very briefly on any individual, he might have recognized him through gait or stance, but his startled agitation did not allow for such careful study. Wrenching himself up on one elbow, he stared in shocked immobility.

Now the night was crammed with the acid sting of threat; this unexpected motion jangled with the harsh clamour of a terrifying unknown. Everything in Scott rang out in silent alarm. Adrenalin pushed and plucked its needles through his flesh. The buzzing of blood in his ears obliterated the soft caress of their feet on the floor as they closed like the mouth of a white flower around Raoul's bed.

Scott raised himself in preparation for a move to help Raoul, but was suddenly – absolutely – halted.

The first of those attacking figures had reached the bedside. Raoul rose in a furious fountain of motion, then paused with one arm extended. For a moment that upraised hand could have signified a warding away, a repulsion (Scott begged himself to believe in this, the frozen instant, the faceless figures, the moonlight on glazed tiles), yet ... not, for the hands that now lifted Raoul's shirt from his body were his own.

Scott fell back onto the pillow, numbed. His brain was fogged with gaudy streamers of colour that mocked the tremblings in his body. This was too much. What did it mean? He did not even want to know, did not want to see anything beyond the flat pointless symmetry of events. Their significance was too terrifying.

The figures slid back from the scene in a white mist. They hoisted Raoul up, sheets pouring from him like water. His suspended body seemed hung, floating on the support of mystery that thickened the air in the room. Then movement injected itself into the blended wall of bodies once more. Raoul, as naked as innocence, was carried down toward the waiting cloakroom door. His upturned face was calm in acceptance. The noiseless procession left only the fragmentary images of devastation; pale limbs, joined hands, reaching arms.

They disappeared through the dark doorway.

Scott, breathing in erratic whistly bursts, could not will himself to look at Anthony's bed. He did not want to know whether it was occupied or not. Shaking, he turned onto his side, taking a last look at Raoul's discarded pyjamas. If he could have done so, he would have removed them with his sight.

Anthony's mother, Mrs Constance Delaney, was, in contrast to her son, a large buxom woman with an untidy beehive of candyfloss hair. Scott saw her for the first time at eight o' clock on the Friday morning as she stepped from her grey Mercedes, wrapped in the heavy leather folds of a stylish coat. She stopped there, hands on the car roof, gazing up at the reformatory as though it had magically appeared before her.

Anthony himself did not move immediately, but continued to stare out of the foyer window at his mother. He and Scott had been waiting there since breakfast had ended, nearly three-quarters of an hour before. Scott felt painfully out of place.

'Come,' Anthony said, as his mother finally began to clip her way across the tarmac. Scott picked up his overnight bag and followed Anthony through the door.

The day was grim and cold, with a sharp wind spilling off the sea. Behind Mrs Delaney the sky was paved with slaty chunks of cloud. Scott shivered in the chill blast of air that arrowed through his clothing.

'Hello,' Anthony said.

'Darling,' breathed Mrs Delaney, and then again, as though she had underplayed the huskiness in her voice on her first try – 'Darling.'

'This is Scott Berry,' said Anthony.

'Darling, you look well.'

Scott was not sure whether this last was directed at Anthony or himself, but he clutched Mrs Delaney's proferred fingers by way of greeting.

'Come on, darling, put your bags in the back and let's go. We've got a long drive ahead of us. Is it always so *cold* here, darling, how do you bear it?'

Looking back through the misted rear window, Scott mused over his last glimpse of the grey stone building, gliding away into the ghostly frieze of peaks. It seemed very different now to how it had looked on his first approach nearly a whole summer before. Scott knew that familiarity did not necessarily breed contempt, but it certainly bred an altered perspective. He turned to face the front.

'My God, but I spent a terrible night last night,' Mrs Delaney cried joyfully. 'The *hotel,* you know! So shabby! But what do you expect here? At the end of the earth, you know, darling.' She drew on her cigarette, then dangled it out of the window in its long green holder.

Johannesburg, more than eight hundred kilometres away in the Transvaal, might as well have been a fragment of eternity.

When Scott looked back on the journey afterward, it lost all sense of time. It seemed almost to have the quality of seasons in succession – from the grey wetness of the coast came a clambering up roads in a green and golden world; then a dropping into an endless plain of heat and yellow dust, and finally a crossing of the autumnal embers and ash of the Transvaal veld. All recollection was bound about by chains of unending speech.

'Darling, Robert will be so thrilled to see you again. Not that Judy and Carol and Neil won't, but Robert has been talking about you for the whole week. Do you know, your uncle Milton got married again! To Gail – you remember Gail, darling? That puggy-looking girl with the moles on her shoulders ... your father says to tell you he's sorry he won't be able to see you this weekend, but he's overseas again. On business. But you'll see him next time. Anyway, Conrad will be home. Now, darling, I know what you think of Conrad, but he *is* my husband, and he's been very good to you. My God, how long is it since you came home? Years, it must be. Do you know, Greta resigned from Anglo-American two months ago? But you haven't met Greta yet, have you, darling ...'

Eleven interminable hours later Mrs Delaney rolled the car down into the cool interior of an underground garage and sighed. 'Home at last,' she said. 'Now remember to be nice to Conrad, darling, and give Robert a warm hello – he's *so* excited you're coming.'

Scott had caught sight of Anthony's home from a hundred metres down the tree-lined road. Set in the deep heart of

Wendywood, it stood above the smaller (yet equally impressive) houses about it. The trimness of the dark tiled roof gave a subtle gravity to the dazzling white riot of walls and windows. Moving up the long brick drive beneath overhanging trees, Scott had experienced an uncomfortable sense of déjà-vu, not in terms of place, but of ambience. This was wealth; this was home; this was homeliness.

Anthony stepped from the car wearily and arched his aching back. Mrs Delaney lit a fresh cigarette and swung the door open.

'Come on, darling,' she said to Scott. 'Make yourself at home.'

A short flight of stairs led up from the garage to the kitchen. His bag pressed against his side, Scott walked up into the cool glow of the overhead lights.

A small boy with tousled black hair and a serious frown on his face was sitting on the table. Behind him were two girls – twins, it seemed – with their salt-white hair braided out behind them. All three studied him without speaking.

'Hello, darlings,' Mrs Delaney said. 'Say hi to your brother and his friend.'

There was no reply.

'That's Neil and Judy and Carol,' Anthony pointed out for Scott. 'This is Scott Berry.'

There was still no answer.

'Darling, why don't you go up to your room and put down your bags? Supper is nearly ready, I'm sure.'

Anthony did not move. Scott, beside him, felt a deep ache as he realized why not.

'Go on, darling. You – oh, my God!' Mrs Delaney raised a shocked hand to her mouth. 'You don't have a room, do you? This is the first time you've come here. How silly of me!' She giggled. 'You'll just have to take the spare room, hon. Judy, be a real darling and show the boys where the spare room is.'

As they moved down a panelled passageway, Scott heard Mrs Delaney's renewed giggles floating after them.

Again – that sense of relived experience. Anthony's head

moving in front of him brought back a crisp picture of another time. The first walk down to the beach. It struck Scott just how much had passed between those two moments.

The spare room was panelled in the same dark wood. Between the two quilted beds a large bay window yielded a view of level lawns. Scott caught a glimpse of a swimming pool and tennis court behind tall plumed fir trees. He put his bag down gingerly on the fluffy blue pile of carpet.

'Very nice,' he said nervously.

'Yes, very nice,' Anthony echoed.

Scott glanced up. Anthony was standing at the window, hands on hips, staring out. Scott could not see his face.

Minutes passed. Finally, Anthony swung round and clapped his hands. 'Sorry,' he said. 'Let's –'

He broke off as a small figure appeared in the doorway. Scott turned to the newcomer. It was a young boy with hair as fine and dark as the surrounding wood panelling. He gazed at Anthony.

'Robert!' Anthony said, dropping to his knees and opening his arms. 'Come here, Rob!'

'Bugger off,' Robert said sullenly.

Conrad Delaney, Anthony's stepfather, was a large man with waves of black hair that crinkled back from his forehead. His face seemed to have been badly formed from separate pendulums of flesh, welded together into a craggy composition, from which deep-set eyes glittered as he shook Scott's hand.

'Pleased to meet you,' he said. 'We're very glad that Anthony has decided to visit us. Hey, Anthony?'

'Yes,' Anthony said.

'Supper's on now, your mother says.' He took a last look around the room; at the night that was beginning to brush against the windows. 'Like it?' he said.

'What?' Anthony looked around as though he had missed something.

'The place. Bit of a change, hey?'

'Yes,' Anthony said.

Mr Delaney stood for a moment, looking at the carpet with a bemused smile on his face. Then he picked up his briefcase from where he had dropped it on entering. 'See you at supper,' he said and went out.

Scott was not, he believed, in the least religious. Yet on Friday night he tossed between dreams that tore his mind with hidden claws: dreams of crying figures nailed to crosses on a hill. Even after he awoke, moaning, in the cold paleness of dawn, the sweat-oiled sheen of those upturned faces, the ruby knots that glistened on their hands, the grating rattle of their clenched teeth, still lingered in his shaken mind. He lay and forced his breath to settle quietly in his chest.

Saturday, despite the cloudless brilliance of the sky, was a grey day.

After breakfast, Scott and Anthony put on their costumes and went down to the pool. As he trod the chlorinated clearness of the water, Scott could remember only the tugging and rushing of the cloudy ocean waves. He felt guilty, but he longed for that familiar sweep of beach. He said nothing as he swam beside the silent Anthony up and down the length of the pool.

They lunched at the poolside on white rolls, cheese and milk. Neither of them spoke during the meal.

That afternoon they went for a walk, a long and again silent stroll through the quiet streets of the neighbouring suburbs. In Morningside they found a small school that displayed its name – Redhill – in large ornate lettering on its facade, tucked away in a side street. They sat on the grass fronting the school grounds, taking temporary comfort in the territory of their peers. It occurred to Scott that had Anthony not been sent to Bleda Reformatory, he might have had to attend this school. It was an unsettling thought.

That night the family ate supper together in the long dining room. Mrs Delaney talked happily of her shopping experiences that morning, of the threatening storms in the western Transvaal, of Greta's success in her new job. Her husband bent over his food, murmuring agreement whenever it was demanded of him.

Anthony climbed wordlessly into bed at half past nine. Scott, who was not tired at all, felt obliged to follow suit. He lay in the dark, listening to his friend's soft breathing from across the room.

When Scott woke, he could not at first remember where he was. Lightning bloomed outside and crusted the interior of the room in stark fluorescence. He saw Anthony's sleeping form. He was in Wendywood, Johannesburg.

Anthony's home.

The bedside clock grinned the time at him: 1.30 a.m. He sat up and threw off the quilt. Outside, lightning spangled the sky again.

There was no sleep left in him. Rising, Scott moved to the window and stood, looking out.

The storm was far away. In the distant sputters of light he could see roiling blue cloud massed against the skyline. The air, though, was sticky even here; it lay heavily on the room. He opened a window and leaned forward into the slight coolness that bled in from outside. There was a faint scent of fertilizer from the flowerbed below.

He could not drive from his mind the recurring image of Raoul being lifted from his bed and borne down toward a doorway. It filled his head with clarity; every line, every pore, standing out for his inner sight. It disturbed him to think of what Raoul had never revealed to him, of how much he had been able to keep hidden.

Yet, there was also a deep fear in Scott: that the scene had taken place only in his mind. Perhaps it had been no more than a vivid dream that he had spawned in his tortured brain. No more than that ... but was that not a more terrible alternative to reality?

'What are you doing?'

Scott jumped at the voice. Turning, he saw Anthony sitting up in bed.

'Can't sleep,' he said.

Anthony studied him for moment longer, then swung free of the sheets and came to stand beside him. They stared out at the approaching storm. Stars were becoming dimmed in the first fuzz of cloud.

'Anthony,' Scott began, then faltered. He hesitated for a second, then tried again. 'Anthony –'

'Look, it's not you, Scott,' Anthony said, gazing out at the brooding garden. 'It's just the change. So different.'

Scott said nothing, but silently urged the words to come from his friend's mouth.

'I don't really know,' Anthony went on. 'I look, but I can't see ... anything. When we were still in Port St Johns, before I came to Bleda, we stayed in a three-roomed shack. Behind a restaurant. My mother used to work in the kitchens.' He bit at his lip. 'I ... shared a bed with my brother. The place stank – we could hear drunks relieving themselves against the wall outside at night. Hell would have been a godsend.' He looked at Scott. 'Then I left for Bleda. My mother wrote to say she'd remarried and they were going to move. I'd met Conrad in the restaurant before – I never hated him. They're wrong, Scott, when they say I hate him. I don't. It's just that he took them all to another world. I've somehow been left behind, that's all.'

Scott looked past Anthony at the stormy sky. His recollection catapulted itself through the years past, through pictures of Raoul and the taste of his commitment. Raoul's form became transparent and colourless against that of Anthony Lord; it faded into greyness. Suddenly all that was important was embodied in Anthony, in the projecting ears, the chestnut hair, those ... eyes. Those goddamned clear blue eyes. Wild dew and winter staring from that face.

'See, you are my friend,' Anthony said. 'My only friend. I like you more than I like myself ... that's how I know. That's the truth. God knows why. Friends are rare. I don't deserve it.'

Raoul's face hung over Scott with the weight and sombre grimness of the night. But as he continued to stare at Anthony, its lines and features wavered and melted. All that was left was this. Anthony and Scott. Wendywood. Johannesburg.

For ever after, when Scott thought back on Anthony Lord, his face would come to him as it was now: turned half away, painted in the gleam of blue lightning. It seemed very far away.

'You must never blame me, Scott, for what I'm going to do today. It seems like I'm betraying you, or something, but I'm not. Maybe it's a sin.' He glanced at Scott and lowered his eyes. 'Yes, of course it's a sin. But ... it hurts too much. I always do things because of how I hurt. Come – I'll phone for a taxi and we'll go to the station. I don't know when the first train to Bleda leaves, but we'll catch it. I'll leave a note for my parents. I can't stay here anymore.' He smiled that broad and unforgettable smile. 'I can't stay here anymore.' Scott never saw that smile again.

The train came swaying into Bleda station at half past six that Sunday evening. Scott and Anthony, wearied into numbness, stumbled off and down the platform. Anthony phoned the reformatory from a grimy booth at the station entrance and Mr Bishop came to fetch them half an hour later.

Driving back down the desolate stretch of coastal road in the warm golden light of a summer evening, Scott felt almost content again. Anthony, quiet beside him, was looking out on the metal surface of the sea.

'Have a good time?' Mr Bishop asked.

Scott felt at a loss for a reply, but Anthony said, 'Loved it.'

When they walked into the dormitory, they were met with silence. Each boy sat on his bed and stared at them.

'Hi,' said Scott, but there was no reply. Moving down to his

117

locker to unpack his bag, Scott saw that William Lee was back with them, fast asleep on his bed.

'Hey,' Raoul said to Scott. 'Weren't you only gonna come back tomorrow?'

'Changed our minds,' Scott said shortly.

'Enjoy yourself?' Raoul put intense interest into his voice. Scott straightened and looked at Raoul. 'Loved it,' he said.

'Arentcha gonna ask me 'bout my weekend?'

'How was your weekend, Raoul?'

'Great, screwball, just great. Guess what – old Mark Archer found a snake yesterday.'

Scott's tone quickened. 'What kind?'

'Yellow cobra. Found it sleepin' on the path down to the beach. Son of a bitch was just waiting for somebody to step on him.'

'What did you do with it?'

'Caught it.' Raoul grinned. 'Markie's got it in a box under his bed, haven't you, Mark?'

Scott opened his mouth, shut it, and opened it again. 'You can't keep a snake in here,' he said.

'Just what I was sayin'.' Raoul looked round the dormitory. 'I was just tellin' the guys how it would be fun to put our snake in Mr Hall's desk drawer.'

Scott felt paralysed from the waist down. 'Raoul, you didn't tell them that,' he said.

'I did. Somethin' wrong?'

'But you can't –'

'It was just a joke, screwball – see? One of those things you laugh at.'

'A joke? Raoul –' Scott broke off as he became aware of the silence in the room. He turned to face them. 'What is it with you?' he said. 'Somebody *talk*, for God's sake.'

Nothing.

'Come on, Scott,' Anthony said. Scott glanced at him. As he started to look away again, his eyes were drawn back to Anthony's face. He was papery in his paleness, his skin sequined with sweat. 'Come on,' he said again.

'Where to?' Scott said, alarmed. Anthony had not unpacked his bag. He stood looking over the bed.

'Just come on, Scott.'

Scott started to obey, hesitated, and looked back. Raoul's eyes were deep, unwavering, black. Scott followed Anthony out of the room.

They walked out of the main entrance of the building into the last light of the late afternoon. Already crimson was beginning to chew at the western fringe of the sky and black was seeping in from the east. They stood for a moment in the thin breeze.

'Do you remember the first day you came here?' Anthony said. 'When we talked on the beach?'

'Yes – I –' Scott frowned in recollection. 'The sea is never, always, and for ever. Was that it?'

'Ah.' Anthony smiled bleakly and began to walk across the lawn. Scott skipped into step with him. They entered the forest and started to move down beneath the long and faded shadows of the trees.

Scott had always loved best this gentle time of day, with its mellow light and soft sky. It was part of him, a visible extension of complacency. He sighed, not unhappily.

A strong spurt of wind battered leaves across their path. Anthony looked down at them absently. Scott could no longer walk beside him, for the path was too narrow, but he kept close behind.

They reached the open shelf where the cliff ran beside the path. Automatically Scott slowed to catch a fuller glimpse of the yawning chasm. For an instant he was buried like a dart in the warm flesh of the dying day, content and calm, a piece of the summer.

Anthony put his hands into his pockets and turned to Scott. He stared at him for a long moment and Scott saw – with a fearful heave inside his chest – that the blue flame had turned to ash in those crystal eyes.

'Scott,' Anthony said, 'you should know that many more things than just the sea are – never, always, and for ever.'

119

Scott knew then what was going to happen and he stretched out his arms. Suddenly – oh, so suddenly – there was a universe contained in two reaching hands and a pair of dead eyes.

After Anthony Lord had jumped from the cliff, Scott hurled himself on his knees at the edge, throwing his eyes down, down, down, for a last glimpse of that body before the life had left it. Too late. Too late.

And then Scott was screaming again, just like when Joseph had fallen onto them from the tree, and he was weeping with tears that burnt out his eyes, tears so acid that they could have come from nowhere other than his heart, his heart, his goddamn bloody fucking heart, because he had just lost all that was beautiful and good, and he had nothing left, nothing, and he wanted death, he wanted to die, but he knew, screaming and weeping, that he was going to endure, he would remain, while all about him the world was falling into ruin.

Scott remembers: being caught once more.

They – he and Raoul and Joseph – have not gone more than ten kilometres when the police van pulls up on the road in front of them. Scott wants to try and bluff it out, but Raoul does not hesitate. He skids desperately down an earthen bank to a long ploughed field. Scott and Joseph follow him, but the cops are piling out of the van in pursuit.

'Split up, split up,' Raoul shouts, and Joseph obeys him, running off to the left. Scott, terrified, stays with Raoul, flying over the furrows.

'Leave me, go away!' Raoul screams back over his shoulder. 'We must split up!' But Scott, though he hears the thump of booted feet behind, cannot force himself to tear away. He just keeps Raoul's dodging back three feet in front of him.

Strangely, it is Raoul, not Scott, that they catch first. Scott sees a familiar blue uniform lunging past him, and then Raoul's back is not visible any more. Scott tries to run on for a way, but then he stops of his own accord and walks back to them.

Joseph has also been caught and is being led off across the field.

Scott and Raoul, each with an arm gripped by a young police officer, follow slowly.

It is their first view of the world from the interior of a police van. The wire grille that keeps them in seems to distort perspective somehow. Objects change their shape, becoming larger or smaller.

By South African law, a children's court may not sit in a room in which a court ordinarily sits. The trio is to be tried in more informal surroundings. They are presided over by a commissioner of child welfare, a title that softens his normal rank of magistrate. The officer delegated by the Attorney-General to conduct prosecutions at the public instance before the court of the Baytown district takes on the role of children's court assistant. He is a friend of Dr Berry's.

The court appoints a probation officer, a young man by the name of Philip Parsons, to investigate the home and background of all three boys. Dr Berry is infuriated at having to answer questions with regard to the upbringing of his son. Mr Parsons finds Raoul's home to be bearable. Joseph, however, is not to be so fortunate. Mrs Hamilton has died barely a year before, and her husband had left her before Joseph turned five, so Joe has been living under the guardianship of a senile grandmother.

The court hears Mr Parsons' report. After listening to each of the boys in turn, the magistrate sentences each of them to four strokes with a light cane for their crime of theft. In addition, he decides that Joseph and his sister should be moved to a place of safety (a house designed for the purpose of housing misguided delinquents) to prevent him from further pursuing the course that he has been taking.

Directly after the sentence has been given, the boys are taken to receive their punishment. Scott doubts that he has ever experienced such pain before. He wishes that the doctor, who is present to examine the effects of each stroke in turn, would de-

cide that he has undergone sufficient reprimand. But with each searing blow the disinterested head simply leans forward, nods, and moves back. The next stroke follows. All the way home, Scott still hears the swish and hiss of descending wood.

His mother, who drives all three of them home, is crying a little as Scott goes silently up to his room. He can still feel the burning welts across his buttocks. He examines the bruises in the mirror, then goes to lie face down on the bed.

Dr Berry comes in, dark with anger. 'Four cuts?' he says. 'A hundred too few. I hope you've learnt your lesson.'

Scott says nothing, but glares up at his father.

'I'm speaking to you,' Dr Berry says. 'Don't get insolent here.'

'What do you want me to say?'

'How about "sorry"?'

'Sorry? For what?' Scott pushes himself up on an elbow. There is a twinge from his bruised backside.

'For disgracing the family! For losing me the esteem of my patients!' Dr Berry breathes noisily.

'Oh, God,' Scott groans, also angry now.

'I said don't be insolent!'

'I wonder,' Scott says, 'how they could have taken Joe to a place of safety, and left me here.'

Dr Berry takes a furious step forward and begins unbuckling his belt.

'Oh no,' Scott says. 'You're not going to hit me now!'

'Do you want to bet on that?'

'Listen, please – wait – I've just been caned with –' Scott sits up and holds out warding hands.

'I don't care! I don't care! How dare you be so cheeky to me, you little –' Dr Berry swings with the belt and it wraps its length with a crack around Scott's torso. Pain flares again. With a cry, Scott rises.

The next lash curls around his buttocks and bites into fresh wounds. This time Scott screams and tears begin to flood his eyes.

'Crying now?' Dr Berry swings again. 'Not so big now, eh?

Friends can't help now, eh? Not so big n–'

He becomes abruptly silent as Scott hits him.

The blow is not a heavy one, but it splits Dr Berry's lip open. Aghast, stunned, he steps back, touching disbelieving fingers to his mouth.

Scott punches him again, and this time there is force behind his fist. Dr Berry staggers, dropping his belt.

'Wait –' he cries.

'No,' Scott says, and sends a final blow to his father's jaw. Dr Berry goes down on his backside, glassy-eyed. Blood spatters his stupefied face.

Scott, still quivering with anger, seizes his coat from a chair and strides out. As he goes down the stairs he feels light-headed and nauseous. There is no going back now.

He finds Raoul fast asleep on the couch in his flat. Scott pushes him awake gently. He sits up.

'Scottie?' Raoul says. 'What are you doin' here? I thought your father said –'

'Forget my father,' Scott says. 'I've just hit him. I can't go back.'

'You – no, you're jokin'.'

'I'm not.'

'You hit him? You hit your dad? Swear?'

'Yes.'

Raoul begins to laugh.

'What's so funny?' Scott is ruffled at this response.

'I've been wantin' to do that to your old man ever since I met him. Remember when you introduced me to him – we was busy drinkin' wine at your house an' he came in – an' I said, "Hello, Mr Berry"? Remember what he said? "I'm Doctor Berry, young man!" Stupid old tit!'

'No, he isn't,' Scott says angrily.

'What are you shoutin' about, screwball – you hit him.' Raoul stands up. 'So what're we gonna do now?'

Scott looks down at his hands. 'Let's go, Raoul,' he says. 'Let's go off again. We can get to Durban, get on a ship. God, Raoul, there must be peace somewhere. We've got to find it.

Maybe an island, far away from other people –'

'Joe too?'

'… Yes, Joe too.'

Raoul grins down at him. 'Let's not get caught this time.'

'Sure.' Scott shakes his hand. 'Let's get going.'

'Wait a second – where are we gonna find Joe?'

Scott hesitates momentarily. 'Let's go quickly,' he says. 'He's probably still at home now.'

He is, but he is not alone. Mr Parsons is there as well.

Joseph and Mr Parsons stare at Raoul and Scott. Nobody talks for some while.

Raoul looks around and sees Joseph's half-packed suitcase on the table. Barbara is crying. The grandmother is nowhere to be seen. Scott sees Raoul's face tighten and recognizes it as a dangerous sign.

'What are you two doing here?' Mr Parsons says. He looks confused.

'We've come to take Joseph,' Raoul says, stepping forward and closing the door behind him.

'No need,' the foolish Mr Parsons assures him. 'I'm here to do that.'

'You arsehole,' Raoul says. 'Just keep out of the way. Got your stuff, Joe? Got some cash?'

'Wait a minute here,' Mr Parsons protests weakly.

'Shut up, screwball. Let's go, Joseph.' Raoul has his hands on his hips.

'What about Barbara?' Joe says.

'Leave her. Watcha want with her?'

'I can't leave her, Raoul. They'll take her away. She's my sister.' Joseph throws a glance at Scott.

'He's right, Raoul.' Scott takes Barbara by the hand. 'We can't leave her.'

'So bring her, then,' Raoul says. 'Watcha waitin' for?'

'Come on,' Scott says, starting for the door.

'Hold it right there!' Mr Parsons makes a last grab at authoritarianism. Raoul laughs delightedly at him, and he blushes.

'Say somethin'?' Raoul asks sweetly.

'You boys had better think twice about this,' Mr Parsons advises, sweating visibly.

'You gonna stop us, screwball?'

'I –'

Raoul takes a threatening step towards him.

Mr Parsons has obviously read an account of the sinking of the Birkenhead. He flattens himself across the doorway. 'You're not going anywhere,' he whispers desperately. 'It's my duty to stop you –'

Raoul knees him in the groin. As he doubles over with a high-pitched cry, Raoul pushes him away from the door and opens it.

But Mr Parsons has set his heart on dying. Still bent over and clutching the afflicted area, he bounds Quasimodo-like into their path once again.

This time it is Scott who takes great pleasure in striking him. Mr Parsons falls back and as he slumps Joseph wallops him across the neck for good measure.

The doorway, now, is undefended.

'Free at last,' Raoul says.

They are caught three days later in Port Shepstone by a passing police van.

When Scott took his first walk after Anthony's death – nine days before – the matron watched him anxiously from the window of her room.

He was weak from the time that he had spent in bed and the sedatives that had been administered to him, but there was a new glitter in him. He had sensed it when he looked up at the sky from his bed and, seeing the blue dome scattered with torn scraps of cloud, felt an old urge to look out at the sea. That was the only reason he had got up that morning.

Scott stood for a moment at the head of the stairs which led down from the reformatory entrance. The scene was still the same to his disappointed eyes: he had expected – half hoped for – a change of some sort. Perhaps nothing as momentous as a shattered mountain or a burnt out landscape, but ... just something ... to acknowledge .... Yet here the world continued to spin, unchecked, undisturbed. Even the gulls still slid along the shivering air on upheld wings.

He started down the lawn, hands thrust deep into the slit pockets of his cardigan. Moving down the path, he recalled exactly every step he had taken nine days before.

At the cliff edge he walked on with hurried steps, looking straight ahead. Ocean swells carved the rushing surface and whitecaps marked the wind, much further out.

There were boys lying on the sand below and Scott slowed his pace. He had no wish to mix with them now. The thought of conversation was sickening to him. Where to run?

... the bluff ...

Suddenly the dark and mysterious promontory was appealing in its solitude. Scott veered off at an angle through the drunkenly-leaning trees and vanished into the coolness.

The wind on the bluff was strong and gusty. It lifted his fringe from his forehead. Pushing his hands forward again in his pockets to stop the cardigan's wild flapping, Scott walked out along the sparsely grown spine which marked the margin of the bay.

At the furthest point he stopped, breathing deeply. Even the air tossed here in collusion with the deep water churning at the foot of the drop before him. The rock falling away at his feet was riven and black. Nearer the base, upon which the incoming waves beat relentlessly, it glistened with spray. The cliff here easily doubled the height of the other next to the pathway.

The horseshoe curve of the bay now lay to Scott's left. He could even make out the distant figures of boys in the surf. Turning to the other side, he looked on the shoreline running towards the town of Bleda, eventually growing hazy with distance. The broken hills and gullies continued inland. No human being was in sight.

He stood, far above the wild and empty beach. There was

nothing habitable in it, yet it beckoned to him. He did not move.

Looking down once more, he saw a gash of boiling surf on the ocean surface. It could only be the reef. He recalled then how Anthony had pointed out beyond the bluff on their first day at Bleda and he felt a renewed ache in his chest at the memory. Anywhere, at any time, he could not escape the past. Ghosts do not have to be visible to haunt the endless present.

And whatever Anthony had said, it had been a betrayal. It was a denial of all feeling; an act of coldness, ignoring all question of need and loyalty and faith. No greater blow could have been struck if Anthony had told him it would be better not to speak to one another again. There was nothing left to Scott: not peace, not joy, not content. Walking through his brain with the passing of every second came a figure whose extended paces made their own tacit mockery of his stature.

No peace, no joy. No content. Never again.

A dry rattle attracted his attention and he turned. Beside him, standing no higher than his waist, was a small tree, reaching its longing branches for the sun. Scott knelt to touch it, and saw that it was hung with tiny closed buds. Not one of them was open, but he sensed that they enclosed a hidden beauty.

God looked on all that he had made and saw that it was ... good. Good.

He rose and looked down on the stunted tree, knowing that it could have grown to tower far above him if it had taken seed in more protected ground.

Good? No, not good. Scott put his hands in his pockets once again and turned to the sea. He had used to think in terms of good and evil, but not any more. He had thought Anthony Lord was a good person, but no longer. He had simply suffered, that was all; he had lived and suffered and died. There was nothing good in life. There was only suffering and evil, no more than that. Suffering and evil.

He stood for a while longer, feeling the extent of his loss. It seemed strangely unjust that the human system made no place for majesty: all that Anthony Lord had ever stood for, the fabric of his dreams and woes, the very substance of his soul – this total immensity had shrunk in the space of three seconds to the size of an obituary notice in the local newspaper.

The injustice, to Scott, was even greater, for it encompassed his own life as well. Gazing on the new bleakness in himself, Scott knew that far far more than Anthony Lord had died nine days before.

He flexed his forearms, then relaxed. Slowly he became aware that he was weeping, the tears running in a salty stream from his eyes. He could taste them on his lips.

And – oh, God! the *agony* of those silent hanging buds in the wind off the sea.

Mr Hall sent for Raoul and Scott early that evening. They were both showering at the time; dressing quickly, they went down to the study, their hair still sodden.

Mr Hall, as he called them in, seemed strangely disturbed. His face was suffused and his hands shook.

'Sit down, both of you,' he ordered. Scott detected a tremor in his voice.

Mr Hall looked directly at Raoul. 'Seen this before?' he asked, and threw something across the desk. It was a dead snake, bleeding from several crushing blows across its back. The lidless eyes still stared.

'That's Mark Archer's cobra,' Scott said. Mr Hall, at the sound of his voice, glanced over at Scott, but then fixed his gaze on Raoul once again.

'This was in my drawer,' Mr Hall said. 'It was alive then.'

'So?' Raoul said.

'Nothing. Nothing at all.' He sat back. 'I just wanted to show it to you.' He breathed deeply. 'Mark Archer has admitted to putting it there.'

'So what d'you want me to –'

'I said, *nothing*.' Mr Hall's voice was sharp. 'I have had

Mark Archer sent to an observation centre.'

'What's that got to do with me?' Raoul crossed his legs.

'Mark Archer said that he did it at your instigation.'

'That is a lie!' Raoul half rose and shouted. 'That is a god-damn bloody lie! Why should I –'

'It's true, Mr Hall,' Scott said quietly. 'Raoul did suggest it.'

Mr Hall put his head to one side and opened his eyes fully.

'You jerk,' Raoul said with controlled violence. 'You dirty rotten filthy little prick.'

'It's true, Raoul, you know it's true.' Scott looked up at him.

'Friend! Ha! I thought you were my friend. So much for friendship.' Raoul sat down and slowed his breathing. 'It's a lie, Mr Hall, I swear it's a lie. Scott wasn't even there. I was trying to cover up, but I'll have to be honest now, I see. I swear this is true, Mr Hall, no lies .... look, what actually happened was that Spencer Hardy suggested it. I swear it! I tried to protect him, him bein' a friend and all, but it looks like that won't help now –'

'Oh, yes. Talking of Spencer,' Mr Hall said. 'He tells me he has received a note threatening his life.'

'This is gettin' borin', but what's that gotta do with me?'

'He tells me that the note could only have come from you.'

'Liar!'

'He says that you have made repeated verbal threats to him.'

'Liar! He is a liar, Mr Hall –'

'That may or may not be so, Dean – I do not care, either way. It seems I have lost control of this situation, but I shall regain it. I don't want to listen to your stories now –'

'But I have to –'

'Be quiet. I have wasted enough time.' Mr Hall steepled his fingers under his chin. 'The reason I called you in here was to tell you that you are being released on licence on Friday.' He stared pointedly at Scott. 'Both of you,' he added.

'Licence?' Raoul was stunned. 'You can't just –' He

blinked. 'Look, only people who deserve it, people who're *good*, are let out on licence.'

'Well?' Mr Hall tapped his fingers on the desk.

'So – I don't deserve it. This jerk, maybe –' he indicated Scott – 'but not me.'

'I'll be the judge of that.'

'You know what I've done here. You're just scared that the world will see you can't handle this .... You know what I've started up.' Raoul was on his feet again.

'What, Dean?' Mr Hall's voice was stony as he glared at Raoul.

Raoul mouthed an incoherent reply, then sank back into his chair. 'Please –' he said.

'You're leaving on Friday.' Mr Hall relaxed. 'You may both get out of my study now.'

'Why?' Raoul's jaw was set. 'Why all of a sudden –'

'I've stood this long enough.' Mr Hall rose. 'Get out of my study!'

Raoul stood up with fury, flinging over the chair as he did so.

Mr Hall said nothing as he crossed the room and slammed the door behind him.

Scott stirred then. 'Why both of us, Mr Hall?'

Eugene Hall shook himself out of some private reverie. 'That is my decision,' he said.

'Yes, but why? I've done nothing –'

'That's exactly why. You understand, a period in a reform school is designed to shock the misguided individual – two years is only a provisional sentence. For any length of sentence, if the person concerned has not been released on licence after two years, I am required to write to the Minister to explain why not. So you see, most of you should be out on licence fairly soon. You have every opportunity to earn it. You, Berry, have been here for a whole summer, and you've proved your worth. It's time you got your chance.'

'Yes,' Scott murmured, head down. 'There's nothing for me anymore. I have no place left in the world. There is no place for me here. I don't really understand what I am to do.'

'Go home,' Mr Hall said. 'I've looked at the probation officer's report. Your parents are wealthy, you have a lovely home. There is everything you need there. There is love for you at home, Berry.'

'I at least know that it isn't enough to love in this world, Mr Hall.' Scott looked up. 'And you've never called me Berry before.'

'Well, I'm sorry, Scott.' Mr Hall picked up the dead snake from his desk and dropped it into a plastic bag.

'Mr Hall, if you've read the probation officer's report, you know that my father doesn't want me back.'

'Well, that's very strange, Berry, because I phoned him today and he said he would try again with you. He is, in fact, coming to fetch you and Dean on Friday afternoon.'

'Why did you give up with Raoul, Mr Hall? Why didn't you have him transferred if you felt –'

'I don't have to explain my actions to you.' Mr Hall dropped the plastic bag containing the snake into the dustbin, and looked up. 'You may also leave my study.'

'I don't understand, Mr Hall.'

'Just get out.'

Scott shut the door behind him softly. Raoul was in the passage.

'You an' me, screwball, are not friends any more.'

'How tragic,' Scott said. 'Excuse me as I grieve.'

'Big words, huh? Where'd you learn them – from that midget who went cliff-jumpin'?'

'Talking of midgets, Raoul ...'

'Watch it, screwball! Just watch it.'

'Yes, I'd better.' Scott folded his arms. 'I should remember the notes that Spencer Hardy got –'

'You know goddamn well why I'm doin' what I'm doin' to Spencer Hardy. He killed Joe. He killed Joe!' Raoul stepped back. 'It doesn't worry you, but it sure as hell worries me!'

'Yes, Raoul.' Scott started to walk away, but Raoul caught at his arm.

'Listen here, screwball. Know why Mr Hall is throwin' you outta here?' Scott turned. ''Cos while you were snivellin' in bed last week, I sent him an anonymous note. Know what it said? It said that you'd told your buddies how you'd pushed Anthony Lord over the cliff.' Raoul laughed. 'Pushed him.'

Scott seized Raoul by the front of the shirt and wrenched him against the wall. What Raoul saw in his face Scott did not know, but he was pale in sudden fear. For a moment Scott stood rigid, trembling with the impact of some deep inner explosion. He knew then that he could break Raoul's face open with his hand, strike him down, leak blood ...

Scott released Raoul and walked away down the passage. There was a chill tingling through his body.

Scott knew that Mr Hall had released Raoul on licence to preserve his own image. He could not bear to admit defeat, so he pretended it had not occurred. When the government inspection took place at Bleda Reformatory that weekend, there would be nothing to alert suspicion. All would be running smoothly. Everybody would be gentlemen. Everything would be homely.

If the building was still standing by then.

Eugene Hall told Mr Bishop that same Wednesday evening of the proposed release of Scott and Raoul. They discussed the whole question in Mr Bishop's study. It seemed strange to Mr Bishop that Raoul should be given the opportunity of licence, but Mr Hall was adamant.

He left Mr Bishop's study at seven o'clock. Feeling vaguely satisfied for the first time in many months, he walked through the downstairs foyer on the way back to his own study.

It was then that he smelt the first acrid traces. His stomach tautening, he lengthened his pace. When dark streamers of smoke came trickling past him, he started to run. But he knew already what he would find.

From the top of the corridor he faced his study. Smoke was spilling from around the edges of the closed door and Mr Hall thought he could see tiny flames spurting behind.

'Fire!' he bellowed. 'Fire, fire!'

He ran down the corridor and tugged frantically at the door. It swung open, blurting heat and flame, and Mr Hall jumped back.

Fire was bubbling crimson across his carpet, coiling up the legs of his desk and clutching lemon fingers at the walls. His bookcase – those beautiful beautiful books! – was fiercely ablaze. It stood like a slab of richly coloured coral against the wall. Smoke filled the room in dense, oily clouds.

Mr Bishop, walking through the foyer en route to the dining room, heard Mr Hall's shouts and began to sprint. At the corner to the corridor, Mr Hall came running past him, sobbing blindly, hands outstretched. Mr Bishop looked back at him, then ran on.

Using the fire extinguisher that hung on the wall outside the study, Mr Bishop began to hose the room with subduing foam. In barely five minutes the blaze had been reduced to hissing steam and ash.

Mr Bishop surveyed the interior of the once attractive study. The carpets were rotted through with blackness; the curtains had shrivelled away; the bookcase was burnt into an unengraved tombstone. The walls, too, once white in their homeliness, were discoloured and cracked. Even through the diffused vapours of rising smoke, these remains were not remotely pleasing to the eye.

Mr Bishop gave the fire extinguisher to one of the curious boys who had come to investigate the disturbance, told him to keep a watch on the room, and went to find Mr Hall. He walked back to his own study, then to the dining room, then to the masters' lounge. He was nowhere to be found.

'Where is Mr Hall?' he asked one of the passing boys.

'I saw him going down to the garage, sir.'

The boy was mildly surprised to see Mr Bishop run off at the speed that he did.

Mr Bishop found Eugene Hall facing Scott across his car.

'You can't leave, sir, please,' Scott was pleading. 'He'll be king of the castle if you do, sir, please –'

'Leave?' Mr Bishop was stupefied as he stepped down into the garage.

'I'm going,' Mr Hall said. Tears were still running down his face. 'I'm going.'

'Why?' Mr Bishop spread his hands.

'He's going to kill me!' Mr Hall cried. 'Raoul Dean! He's taken my dog, my daughter, now he wants me!'

'He doesn't want anybody,' Mr Bishop said soothingly.

'He wants me, I tell you! The boy is an animal! He's taken this place and changed things ... and ... I don't know, but I'm going.'

'You can't Mr Hall,' Scott cried. 'He'll have the whole place to himself then! Please stay!'

Mr Hall swung down into his car and started the engine.

Mr Bishop made a last despairing grab at the hood as he reversed, but nothing would have stopped Eugene Hall then.

Scott felt a hollowness inside himself as he watched the twin beams of the headlights jaundice the vast wilderness of sea and sky and stone ... then vanish.

Scott remembers: the final conviction.

They are tried once again in a children's court. A new probation officer, however, has been appointed to investigate their case. Scott, although he has not returned home, knows that his father does not want him back. Scott's mother is present at the trial, but she does not speak to her son.

The case is soon at an end. Justice van der Westhuizen observes that it is clear no punishment hitherto applied has had the least effect on the three individuals concerned. He adds that this is the strangest case of persistency that he has yet seen in the world of juvenile crime. It is also made clear by Justice van der Westhuizen that while he could perhaps understand the position of Raoul and Joseph who have been raised under 'unfor-

tunate circumstances', Scott, who has had every advantage afforded by a good home and family, has acted in an unforgivable manner.

Scott longs to tell him that people are stronger in their influence than circumstance.

Justice van der Westhuizen concludes that, after due consideration of the situation, he sees no alternative to sending all three boys to Bleda Reformatory. All of them are under sixteen years of age, so by law they are compelled to remain in the reformatory until they are eighteen. Bleda, Justice van der Westhuizen assures them, is renowned for its success in correcting the negative direction that youth occasionally takes of its own accord. 'And,' he says with a wry smile, 'I am positive that once they have been suitably corrected, these three young men will be perfectly acceptable to the ordered society we live in today.'

PART III

The first thing that Scott saw when he awoke was the square vision of sky carved out by the window of the dormitory. Dawn had not yet come, though it was near, and greyness was clustered in the spaces between the stars. Scott sat up.

He felt immediately that he had been sweating. His pyjama top had hiked into sodden fists in each armpit. The sensation was uncomfortable and he took off his shirt. The coolness was soothing.

Thought came almost as a violation of his tranquillity: this was the last full day that he and Raoul would spend at Bleda. Scott's fingers clutched at the sheets in a hybrid confusion of elation and dread. The following day, after school, Dr Berry would be there to sweep them back to the bosom of the normal world. It was fitting that it should be a doctor who would re-instil sanity into existence; healing was his task. Yet Dr Berry's arrival lay beyond the boundary of credible expectation. Today still had to be survived.

There was nothing, now, to hinder the inevitable. All hope of direction had gone when Anthony and Mr Hall had run away.

Mr Bishop, the night before, had made frantic phonecalls to a number of authorities. The outcome of these was Mr Bishop's appointment as temporary principal until the situation could be investigated. Scott had noted, though, how Mr Bishop had reported the fire in the study as a 'regrettable accident'.

Scott stood up and tiptoed over to the window. Standing with his hands flattened along the sill, he looked out. The sea, beneath the first weals of light that were ridging the sky, lay quiescent and grey. Nearer at hand, the downward-flowing slopes and forests of the visible coastline seemed to have been crudely hewn from masonite; faint glimmers of colour were woven into this drab cloth. Scott raised his eyes to the far horizon where charred logs of cloud were lying in an unsettled heap above the water. A cold wind kissed at him with gentle suddenness, raising gooseflesh across his chest. Withdrawing a little distance from the chill air, he looked up at the window.

The area above it that had been burnt was now repainted; nothing of the underlying blackness could be seen. Two coats of paint had hidden all damage.

Looking now on impassionate and cold surfaces of plaster and brick, he felt a resurrection of old and sleeping nerves. The world, swinging on into space, shrugged its people from it and retained the places of their past. There was nothing more painful than to be able to see and touch the very stone that Anthony had seen and touched, and know that he had dissolved beyond the contact of those brittle reaching fingers.

Shaking free of thought, Scott turned slowly away from the watery light that was flooding more strongly through the dew-cemented window. He climbed back into bed and lay staring up at the ceiling. His attention drifted back to the events of the evening before.

He did not know how, but when he returned to the dormitory after Mr Hall had gone, the other boys already knew that he and Raoul were to be released on licence. He presumed that Raoul had told them. The memory was very strong – he could see their silent, brooding faces as they sat on their beds and watched him from hooded eyes.

He feared them, his peers. Yet … was not the distant future far more terrifying than the near? Scott gave an inward shiver as he considered the prospect of life at home. Whatever Dr Berry had said to Eugene Hall on the telephone the day before, Scott knew that forgiveness was not on his father's list of virtues.

'Awake already, screwball?' Raoul's voice hacked at Scott's contemplations.

'Yes. Too early?' Scott pushed himself up on his elbows. Raoul was sitting on the edge of his bed, looking at him. His hair was tangled from a night of sleep.

Or half-sleep. Scott recalled Raoul's unresisting figure being lifted from the bed ... he forced his mind away from it. That was past. That was over. Or – would be.

'Not too early.' Raoul scratched his chest and grimaced. 'Where's your shirt?'

'I took it off. I was hot.' Scott pulled the sheets aside and put his feet to the cold floor. 'I thought,' he said tentatively, 'that you weren't speaking to me any more.'

Raoul smiled. 'I've thought about that,' he said. 'What's the time? Six o'clock. Christ. Okay, let's go grab a shower before the rising bell.'

Scott followed Raoul into the cloakroom. In the doorway he paused as the lights glimmered on down the length of the room. Steel and plastic shone.

'Remember when we came here the first day?' Raoul was moving down towards the first shower. 'Remember you an' me an' Joe? Seems years ago, hey?' He turned back to face Scott. 'It's 'cos of that that I'm still talkin' to you now. 'Cos we've done a lot together. Dontcha remember, Scottie? At home – before. When we .... Good times we've had, Scott. Good times we've had.' He looked at Scott. 'We were friends, Scottie. You can't change that. You an' me were friends.'

Scott said nothing as he walked down to the shower booth beside Raoul's. He took off his pants and stepped through the curtain. Raoul's voice still carried over the noise of water.

'Jesus – this water is hot, hey? Wakes you up. Listen, Scottie, whadda you say we go back to the old places when we get home? Huh? The trees an' stuff behind your yard? Remember? Scottie?'

'Do you *want* to go home, Raoul?' Scott asked, soaping his legs.

'Do I want to? What does it sound like, screwball?'

'Well, it didn't sound like it when Mr Hall spoke to you last night.'

A silence followed. Scott began to work his fingers firmly

140

over his shoulders and chest, holding his upturned face into the hot stream of water.

Raoul cleared his throat. 'Why do you think I'm talkin' like this if I'm not lookin' forward to goin' home?'

'I thought maybe,' Scott said, 'you were talking like that to find out whether *I* wanted to go back or not.'

The silence, this time, was longer. Scott held motionless fingers splayed over his belly and felt the quiver of held air. Under the running water his uneasy eyes moved toward the next door booth.

'That's what I thought, Raoul,' he said.

No reply.

Raoul's head appeared suddenly over the dividing wall between the booths. Scott was startled at the lidless ferocity of his stare and the hard line of his chin. In the steamy gloom, his tiny figure obscurely resembled some soft white moth dragging itself with absolute effort and concentration from its chrysalis. They looked at each other for a long moment.

'Listen, Scottie,' Raoul said at last, 'I don't know what's gone wrong with us.'

Scott began to rub soap across his shoulders for a second time.

'Hear me, Scott? Hear me, huh?'

'How can we know why things happen between people?'

'We can fix it, Scottie. We're friends, right?'

His voice shouldering through a bright and tangible vision of a pair of crystal eyes, Scott said thickly, 'Yes.'

'I do things I don't mean, Scott – but it's okay. Huh? Huh?'

'Yes, Raoul, it's okay.'

'Look, I'm sorry, Scottie, for givin' Mr Hall that note. You know, the one that said you pushed –'

'Yes, I know which one you mean, Raoul.'

'He prob'ly didn't believe it anyhow. You're too good to have done that, an' everyone knows it. You're a good person.'

'Thank you, Raoul.'

'Come on, man, Scottie – just talk to me. Like you used to. Like before.'

'Would you say, Raoul, that Anthony Lord was a good person?'

Raoul dropped his eyes swiftly. He scratched absently at the top of the wall, not looking at Scott.

'I was speakin' to Mr Bishop,' he said. 'I was just askin' about the people here, y'know? We got to talkin' about Anthony Lord. Know why he was in here, Scottie? Didja hear why he got sent to this place? He set fire to a police station. He threw a firebomb at a policeman. How's that grab you, Scottie? He tried to murder a man he'd never seen before.'

In spite of himself, Scott was deeply shocked; not at the act, but at the thought that must have lain behind it. It seemed an absolute contradiction to him that Anthony, who had been so concerned with the inner tumult of the spirit, should have ever been moved to violence by the physical and material.

Coolly, Scott replied, 'You still haven't told me, Raoul, whether you think he was a good person or not.'

Raoul blinked. 'Obviously, he couldn't have been if he did that.'

'Is Spencer Hardy a good person?'

'Any person who pushed Joseph off that cliff can't be good.' Raoul waved the steam away from his face.

'And you, Raoul?' Scott stopped soaping himself.

'How d'you mean?'

'Are you a good person?'

'I – well – look ...' Raoul propped his chin on his fist and looked down at Scott. 'Listen, Scottie,' he said, 'I think I should tell you ...'

There was a second of utter quiet in which even the woody crackle of the water slid away. Scott reached up to Raoul with his searching eyes. For an instant – no, a fraction of an instant – he longed to make his reaching physical; a reconciliation of bonded hands. Forgive, forget ... forever.

'Look, I like to say that I'm the one who's started all this trouble here. Y'know, the fires and stuff. I say that it's me, an' everyone's happy to go along with it. But it isn't, Scottie, it isn't.'

Scott twisted off the water slowly, not looking away from Raoul's face.

'It's somethin' else, Scottie; I tell you it is. They – Mark Archer an' Martin Everitt an' the others – they just do it. It's not me. I suggest things, but it's really things they have in them. I tell you, Scottie, it isn't me!'

Scott breathed deeply. 'Adelle?' he said.

'Yes ... I did that, all right. But I still don't think it was *me*, if you know what I mean. It's ... I dunno, but it just happened. All the bad things I do ... just happen. Like I'm forced to do them. I dunno.'

'Attila.' Scott looked down.

'They blame me, Scottie, but I can't help being the way I am. Whatever I do, I didn't create myself, Scottie. I didn't ask to be me. I was made this way.

'By who, Raoul?'

'I dunno if I believe in God. But somethin' made me this way. Somethin' made me.'

Scott stepped out of the booth and began to towel himself. The rough material dragging over his body was a physical reflection of the turmoil that his mind was simultaneously undergoing: against will and want, he was longing for the private prison of his home. There was a new and welcome sense of defined contour to his need. He was a part of a pattern, and his place was waiting for him. Raoul too was a piece of the broken scattered world.

And Scott froze momentarily as he realized the direction of his longing: something inside himself still believed that Joseph was out there, woven into the indestructible fabric of the tall green trees behind his house, the birds in their cage, the sultry streets and sky ....

Raoul stepped out of his booth, dripping with water. He sat down on the step leading up into the shower and gently began to dry his hair, looking all the time at Scott. They did not speak for a time. Scott let his hands fall slack, holding the towel at his side.

Raoul coughed.

'Listen, Scottie – I don't know how to say this ...'

'Just speak, Raoul.'

Then, in Raoul's hesitancy, Scott caught the scent of fear. It was so unexpected in this meek basin of walls and tiles that he gazed at Raoul for a disbelieving minute, as a man might try to catch a second whiff of smoke in a closed building.

'You mustn't blame me, Scottie, for what I'm gonna do today.' Raoul took an uncertain breath. 'It might seem like I'm goin' against you and all the old days, but I'm not. I'm not.'

In his shock, Scott felt words battering up to his mouth. He faced Raoul squarely.

'Tell me, Raoul, do you have pain?' he said.

'What?' Raoul looked startled.

'When you think of Spencer Hardy, does it ... hurt you?'

'What kind of question is that, screwball? 'Course it hurts. You can say what you like, I *know* he pushed Joseph. I know he did it.'

'All right, Raoul – I'm not going to argue with you. But when you think of him, his face, all that ...'

'I've told you, screwball, that's got buggerall to do with my feelin's for him.'

'Yes, okay. Okay. Does it hurt, though, when you think of that?'

'Yes, of course!' The words were vehement. Raoul rose and tied the towel around his waist, still looking at Scott.

'So you do have pain.' Scott also tied his towel around his waist. Without looking at Raoul, he walked up to the door. Then he turned back. 'In spite of everything, you do have pain.'

Raoul did not move as Scott left the room.

Scott could not concentrate on schoolwork that morning. During the industrial arts period he found himself staring absently at the twisted dark whorls set into the light grain of the wood. His hands were idle, or otherwise they picked at the buttons of his shirt.

When the final bell sounded at the end of the day, relief brought new energy to him. He went down with his companions to lunch.

A kind of nervous frenzy seemed to be electrifying his system. He couldn't identify its origin, but its effects were noticeable. He wasn't in the least hungry and left half of his food untouched.

Looking down the length of the table, Scott saw that Raoul seemed to be charged with an equal unsettledness. His hands jittered from fork to plate, then jerked up to smooth his hair, dropped to his lap, then raised to his eating utensils once again. His eyes, too, darted from side to side as he chewed.

After lunch Scott ran upstairs to change into a costume; then he went down to the beach. It pleased him to see that he was the first one there. He spread out his towel on the sand and turned to look at the sea.

The water was choppy and rough, the waves driven onto the shore by a powerful breeze. In addition, the lagoon was full. It had pushed a long and filthy arm of brown water into the bay, discolouring the marble slopes of blue. Above the chipped surface of the bay loomed gargantuan cobras of cloud. They were spreading, slowly leeching freshness and purity from the unobscured sky.

Scott remembered his first day at Bleda and the storm that had risen then. He remembered too how Anthony had said, 'It will rain tonight,' and how he had been wrong. But without doubt it would rain that night.

Scott stepped into the shallow seethings that ran up the beach, flinching as he felt the coldness of the water. Spume was bubbling underfoot. He clutched his shoulders and permitted himself the convention of a shiver. Shreds of foam spattered him with the next gust of wind. He took a deep breath and ran out till the water reached his hips. It was even colder than he had first anticipated, and he gasped aloud at the icy sting of it. As a foaming jade cocoon began to enfold him, he launched himself forward in a shallow dive.

Surfacing on the far side of the wave, Scott could taste grit in his mouth; even the clear water was dirty, it seemed. Striking out in a smooth crawl, he began to head for deeper water. Waves were breaking unexpectedly onto him, corrugated by the broken spurts of wind.

Beyond the line of the breakers, Scott stopped, treading water. His mouth was again full of dirt. He spat. Swells were hoisting and hurling him between their dark green cradles and crests; he beat his arms to maintain his position. The sandbank was no longer here, and he longed for its support.

Facing the shore, Scott could see the distant figures of Mr Bishop and several of the boys standing on the beach. He tried to raise an arm to wave, but the ache in his shoulders prevented him.

Off to the left the open sweep of water was impaled by the formless bluff. Scott glanced up at the high peak of stone, but the small tree, laden with its mysterious buds, could not be discerned at that distance. He looked away. Sighing wistfully, he began to head back for shore.

This last swim was not proving to be satisfying. Grey swells constantly trod his head beneath their surface. Scott could not help remembering the very first time he had swum out from the beach; it was a bitter thought indeed that the same sea, at the same time of day, could be so completely different.

He found the bottom with his feet and waded ashore. The beach was nearly full now, littered with sprawled bodies. He picked out his towel among the many others and lay down on his back.

The rising wind was distinctly unpleasant, but the sun was conducive to drowsiness. Scott laid one arm across his eyes and relaxed.

Slowly ... very slowly ... he became aware of an uncomfortably eerie sensation spreading from his belly. It reached out icy fingers until gooseflesh rashed his thighs and the hair was prickling along his arms. Scott sat up and looked around.

Nobody was paying the least attention to him, yet the sensation persisted. And Scott knew too well what it was.

Foreboding. It was a deep and ominous foreboding that froze the fluid in his spine. It had struck him once before, on the beach just before Joseph had fallen onto them from the tree.

Scott was suddenly afraid, and he did not know why.

He realized afterwards that he must have fallen asleep, because when he next opened his eyes the scene had altered completely. He was one of five boys left on the beach. Mr Bishop was no longer there.

Little sunlight was left, both because of the time of day and because of the impending storm. The whole sky was now covered with thick purple cloud, dragging ungainly black mantis legs beneath it. Winds were gnawing at the beach too, kicking debris along in tumbling clouds.

Scott grabbed his towel and stood, cursing at the bite of flying sand. He shook his head to clear it of sleep. Looking up, he could just see the outline of the bluff through the streaming darkness above.

'Better go up now,' one of the remaining boys advised Scott as he came running past. 'Roll-call in twenty minutes.'

Scott was sure that this was probably the last time that he would ever stand on this beach. He had an impulse to make some sort of personal commemoration to the occasion. He threw his mind back over past events, but without success. Nothing offered itself.

Unless –

Scott ran along the beach to the exposed cliff face where, two weeks before, so many boys had inscribed their names in the soft earth. This time he did not have to struggle to find what he sought.

AGONY.

The word still stood out in blunt letters on the sandy face, looking out impassively on the whirling confusion of the shore. It pained Scott to think that this last reminder might be erased by the oncoming storm. Gently he pulled down a few stray fronds to protect it. The action, as much as seeing the stark letters and all they represented, gave him unexpected comfort. The chill inside him lessened.

Gripping his towel about his neck, he ran down to the pathway and began to follow it up the mountain.

The woods were writhing in the wind, pouring down their leaves in molten streams and gnashing their branches on both sides. Scott bowed his head into the blast as he ran on.

At the cliff edge he paused to take a last reflective look. The view, however, was not clear. Below him the outlines of the beach were blurred with driven sand. There were still two boys down there – who they were Scott could not tell. He turned away and hurried up that last gentle slope to the reformatory building.

It was nearly time for roll-call. He took the stairs two at a time. The others had already left the dormitory. Scott ripped off his costume and pulled on casual clothes. No time was left for a shower, although his face was dry and tacky with salt. After battering his hair into shape with a comb, Scott sprinted to the upstairs lounge.

He was just in time. Mr Bishop had already entered the room with the roll-call book when Scott came breathlessly through the doorway. He took a seat in the centre of the front row, directly facing Mr Bishop.

It was then, looking up at Mr Bishop's weathered face, that Scott became conscious that something was wrong. The foreboding was suddenly a hive of bees in his head. It was here. Whatever was wrong came from this room. Scott tried to moisten his lips.

'Good evening, boys,' Mr Bishop said. 'I'm pleased to see that you're all safe from the storm.' He grinned as a heavy rush of wind thudded into the windows.

Scott glanced up. The light was going fast. Now the crisp ticking of the grandfather clock against the rear wall was muted by the throaty gargle and hiss of the wind.

'This should have been done at our next roll-call,' Mr Bishop continued, 'but seeing that they will be leaving straight after school tomorrow, I would like to wish Raoul Dean and Scott Berry all the best as they leave on licence after a summer at Bleda.' Mr Bishop sought Scott in the crowd and beamed warmly at him through the ensuing – sparse – applause. When it ended, he opened his book and found the place with his forefinger.

'Quiet, please,' Mr Bishop called. 'You'll have to answer particularly loudly today for me to hear you over this wind. Gustav Anderson?'

'Present.'

'Herman Askham?'

'Present.'

As the list continued, Scott felt tension humming more intensely through him. He sat forward, clutching his knees with sweaty hands. *What was it? What was wrong?*

'Scott Berry?'

'Present.'

He sank back as Mr Bishop moved unhesitatingly down the list. More names, more replies. *Why did he feel like this?*

'Bruce Davis?'

'Present.'

'Raoul Dean?'

Pause. Mr Bishop looked up.

'Raoul Dean?'

There was no reply. Mr Bishop tapped his pencil on the book.

'Where is Raoul Dean?'

Craig Draper called, 'Mr Bishop, he was still on the beach when I came up.'

Mr Bishop grimaced. 'The idiot,' he said. 'Is he still there? Never mind, let's go on. Craig Draper?'

'Present.'

Scott, settling back into his chair, felt five hearts begin to beat in his chest. His lower body was paralysed as he listened to the names being read off on the list. Beneath his eye, a nervous pulse began to fidget.

Raoul was not here. Scott knew the origin of his foreboding now. He knew also that he had never felt so terrified in his life before, not even when Joe had fallen onto them. He thought numbly: *please, please, let me be wrong*.

Raoul had not been alone on the beach.

Scott could feel himself swaying dizzily as he listened to Mr Bishop's voice, listening, listening, the words booming through his ears, listening for one name ...

'Derek Graves?'

'Present.'

'Stuart Hailey?'

'Present.'

'Spencer Hardy?'

No answer.

'Spencer Hardy?'

In the silence that followed Scott heard the seconds pelting like hailstones from the clock. The paralysis had spread to his arms and shoulders.

Craig Draper said, 'He was also down on the beach when I —'

Scott's first leap carried him over two rows of chairs, his momentum throwing him into one of the seated masters. As the unfortunate man sprawled backwards, Scott flung himself over the next row, spilling chairs in a wild tumble, broke left, and ran for the door.

Behind him, cries of consternation erupted. He paid them no attention, but skidded around the next turn to the head of the stairs. He slipped on the first landing, dragged himself up with desperate fingers and clattered down the next flight.

The force of his rush carried him on into the corridor wall. Pushing himself away, Scott sprinted down the dimly lit passageway. Incredibly, his footsteps kept time with his heartbeat as he came careening into the entrance foyer.

Reaching out for the doors at the main entrance, Scott

prayed a brief but fervent prayer: please, God, don't let me be too late! Please God!

He burst out into the wind.

Raoul saw Scott leave the beach, clutching his towel around his neck. It was then that the tension started for him.

He did not have fear, though. He had realized that he did not understand his own designs absolutely. He could sense, however, the imminent culmination and release of past hurt. This was his excitement; the head-pounding thrill of anticipation.

Raoul felt a belch lodged hard as a marble in his upper chest. Gently, with the heel of his hand, he began to knead it. At the same time he rose and sauntered across the beach.

At the beginning of the pathway he turned and looked back across the sand. For just a moment he savoured the feel of normality. Then, forcing himself to remain impassive, he moved up between the watching trees.

Spencer Hardy saw him go with the same sense of relief that he had experienced at each of Raoul's departures over the past few weeks. After waiting for a while he himself stood and gathered up his towel.

The storm was lowering fast. The hissing mantles of sand that spun and galloped down the dunes were grey and shapeless shadows in the air. Spencer Hardy had always been disturbed by the frenetic uneasiness of the earth before a storm. He hurried his pace now, half-wishing that he had made use of Raoul's company on the walk up to the reformatory building.

The path was a quiet channel in the movement, and Spencer Hardy took comfort in its comparative peace. Leaves still skittered past and trembled in the air about him, but the wind was diluted here.

It was the dying time of day, where dimness begins to parchment the shapes of trees against the sky. Far far higher up the tower burned its single guiding light. He fixed his eyes on it and began to stride uphill.

The undergrowth was thinning here and the wind streamed through more easily. The chill lent attractive images to Spencer Hardy's mind. He looked forward to a hot shower and supper.

It was only then that he realized how late it was. He made a habit of staying on the beach until everyone had left, but he generally left himself time to shower and relax before roll-call. Not today, however. His spirits fell at the thought. Still, to leave the cold wind would be pleasing enough in itself. He broke into a half-run.

The path veered to the right and he slowed as he saw the cliff edge drawing close. The abyss beyond the edge was becoming murky with darkness. He kept close to the left as he approached the drop.

It was only as he stepped into that vulnerable curve of pathway flanked by the cliff that he became aware that he was not alone. It was a ghastly realization, both in that place and at that time of day, and Spencer froze. No sight, no sound had alerted him; nothing more than a deep premonition. Yet he was as certain of another presence as if it had been confirmed by all of his five senses.

Something was behind him.

He could feel adrenalin searing his body. Shaking, he turned around with reluctance and stared into the wall of trees.

Nothing.

But his trepidation did not leave him. As his eyes scanned the ghostly trunks, there came instead a reinforcement of fear. His notions of hot water and food were suddenly ridiculous in their complacency. He was facing something which threatened him. He could sense malice close at hand.

Something was watching him.

Spencer whirled around on his heels. The woods spun about him, mocking him with their dark and hollow places. There was nothing there.

When the voice came, it was a total justification of the depth of his fear.

'Looking for me, screwball?'

The sound was disembodied, floating to Spencer out of the dimness. It seemed to have its origin in the sky.

'I – where are you?' Spencer stuttered.

There was no reply.

Wind came clawing in a hoarse burst over the edge of the cliff, buffeting Spencer with its blast. As he struggled to keep his position, he strained to hear whether Raoul was still speaking.

'Where are you, where are you?' screamed Spencer.

And on the beating blows of wind, ragged in the rushing air, came that bitter voice again: 'Feel what it's been like for me.'

In a moment Spencer knew what was about to happen. Sheer terror almost paralysed him but, compelling movement into his limbs, he started to run.

Too late.

He did not even see Raoul lunging from the forest, but he felt the impact of his rush. A heavy blow smote the side of his skull, flinging white lights through his head. Reeling back in a vision of tottering trees and swaying ground, Spencer heard a snarling breath filling his ears, and did not know whether it was his own or Raoul's.

For a wild clutching moment of imbalance, his back-flung gaze faced the light ablaze in the top of the tower. It stared at him like an accusing eye. Then his guts were hurled to his head and breath set like concrete in his belly.

It took him fully two seconds to realize that he was falling from the cliff.

Scott hesitated as he reached the head of the entrance stairway. With a single glance, the clarity of which was heightened by innate urgency and fear, he took in the welt of inflamed western sky above the water, the boiling ceiling of cloud, and the roaring carpet of trees below. The discord seemed universal: it echoed the turmoil of his own mind.

Suppressing his tears with held breath, Scott blundered down the stairs and began to run across the lawn.

153

Raoul shrank back from the cliff, his breath gasping raggedly in his throat. The brink was clear now, where seconds before it had been obstructed by the figure of Spencer Hardy. Wind poured into Raoul's sweating face.

It was done. The deed, the act – dreamed of, longed for – was over. He had done it.

Raoul's bulging eyes stared unblinkingly at the drop before them, but they did not see. Blood was driving through his body with violent force and his chest heaved. Spencer Hardy was gone. He was dead.

Some dormant reserve of reason told Raoul with quiet irony that all reason had left him; a triumphant fury of exaltation was on him. Under the illusion that illusion was reality, he succumbed to the buffeting of his excitement. Raoul Dean was beyond challenge, beyond reproach. In the execution of his moral duty, he had become invincible. He stood at the edge of the cliff and screamed aloud in his joy. The sound disintegrated into uncontrolled giggling.

Spencer Hardy, plummeting beyond reaction or recall, had no time to register his own fear. He felt himself strike an outcrop with an impact that seemed to shatter his whole chest painlessly. Then, as he slipped on into the maw of gravity again, flames scorched his consciousness away and he sank into whirling darkness.

The next amazed thought to enter his brain was that he had the ability to think. His surprise was detachedly intense: he was still alive. He was alive!

And no longer falling.

He was no longer falling. Further than that, he knew nothing. Sensation had left his body. He could feel no support or direction.

Perhaps, then, this was death. A nerveless motionless state of existence, where the soul is sewn into the heart of unending darkness. Perhaps he was not alive after all. Perhaps he had died.

Experimentally, Spencer shifted a limb. There was no pain, no feeling at all, but he was aware of a rasping in his shoulder that coincided with the movement. He could not, then, be dead. So why had his sight left him?

He blinked forcibly three times; the effort slammed doors in his head. Trickles of liquid spilled down his cheek and a shivery remnant of vision returned to him. He rolled his head, and the blood that had filled his eye-sockets spilled from his face. His jaw felt loose.

Looking up from where he lay on his back, Spencer saw branches tangled overhead. He had fallen through the trees to the ground. He had lived.

He twisted over onto his side with infinite slowness. Things were bursting and breaking in him with the slightest of movements, but they gave him no pain. A dull and rubbery numbness filled his body. Opening his mouth, Spencer let three teeth fall onto the sand. Fresh blood dribbled down over his chin.

He started to claw himself up to his feet.

Raoul could not have cared whether any other eyes saw him at this moment. He was released; he was avenged. This was the end of it.

Still trembling in the delirium of excitement, he started to move away from the cliff. His consciousness was focused on his inner world, but still sufficiently alert to tell him that he was walking down the path towards the beach. A moment later he realized the direction of his hitherto buried purpose: he was going to find Spencer Hardy's body. He was going to look on the destruction he had caused and revel in his confirmed power to subvert his own suffering.

Giggling again, rubbing the sweat from his forehead across his neck and shirt, he started to skip in his excitement.

Spencer Hardy had managed to reach a standing position when he heard Raoul coming.

His shuddering body was half-bowed on its feet, torn by crippling sensations through all its flesh and bone. He could see the peculiar angle at which his left arm dangled, and the huge chunk that had been ripped from his upper torso, but still no pain broke through to his foggy mind.

He heard Raoul giggle.

Spencer snapped up his head and started violently. He knew instinctively that, if he loved life, he must run.

Hobbling, Spencer Hardy began to stumble lamely through the trees to where the clean beach beckoned in the last light.

Raoul found the hollow where Spencer's body had fallen. He saw the pools of oily blood shining back at him beneath the trees.

He began to cry through clenched teeth, beating his frustrated fists against his thighs. Gone was the power, gone the triumph. Exaltation in ashes.

If anybody had been present to observe his kneeling form beneath the wind-rocked trees, they would have seen disbelief in his features. It seemed to Raoul the supreme unfairness that when he placed his trust in the devices of nature his aims should fail. Gravity had not done her work.

He knew that Spencer Hardy had survived the end constructed for him purely to prolong Raoul's suffering. The mockery would never end, even though it was not voiced. Not while Spencer Hardy lived.

Rising suddenly, hands set on his hips, he rocked back and shrieked up to the clouds, 'I'm gonna get you, you prick! Here I come, ready or not!'

Giggling again in renewed anticipation, Raoul began to follow the furrowed trail of blood through the trees.

Spencer heard Raoul's voice and, whimpering in terror, he redoubled his limping pace over the sand.

Dizziness was kindling stars in his head now, and twinges in his limbs heralded the return of feeling to his body. As he caught himself swaying on his feet, he raised his head and saw the jetty before him. Beyond it, a wilderness of black water sighed.

Spencer Hardy – suffering – felt an overwhelming urge to step off that beckoning pier, away from Raoul and worlds and men and pain, into the eternal sea.

Raoul, beneath the trees, continued to bound along the bloodied track of sand. His hands were shaking in an enactment of his intention. 'I'm gonna get you,' he sang out. 'I'm gonna get you!'

His head dropped as he moved, against his will; and then the sweet hot stench – scent! – of blood struck into his nostrils like the sharp edge of a blade. Delirious in its warm and maddening odour, Raoul loped from beneath the trees, doubled over as he inhaled with all his being the fragrance of suffering.

Scott reached the forests that fringed the lawn and ran along their perimeter until he found the path. His heart was juddering as he flung himself down between the trees.

He reached the cliff edge with sweat running into his eyes. Frantic, he bent to the ground to examine the grooves of Spencer Hardy's heels at the brink. He swallowed, pushing his knuckles into the earth to still the trembling of his hands. For some while he could not bring himself to move forward. He shook.

Then sound trickled upward from the foot of the cliff and Scott was freed.

He ran down the path.

Raoul lifted his head as he ran and saw Spencer at the sea edge. For a moment he slowed his pace, not understanding the implication of this new direction of flight, but then he snarled with full realization and began to sprint.

Spencer felt his consciousness draining from him, blackness

spattering his mind. He fell to his knees in the wet sand, head hanging. Six feet away, watery in his fading vision, the jetty loomed black as the gateway to Hell. He strained towards it, but fell forward onto his face. Blood filled his mouth in a silty gush.

'I've got you!' screamed Raoul, running down the last slope towards the jetty. 'I've got you now!'

Spencer heard him and pulled his gummy face from the sand. Drooling crimson from slack lips, he began to crawl towards the jetty.

'You can't get away!' Raoul cried. 'I've got you!'

Spencer reached the beginning of the jetty and crawled with sudden strength. The sea invited, invited ... he was almost at the edge. He was almost there....

He fell forward, exhaustion lashing him. The impact as he struck the planking smashed darkness into his skull. He rolled into unconsciousness. Then pain roared up his left arm, igniting his nerves. Crying out, Spencer opened his eyes.

Raoul reached the jetty and moved down towards his tormentor.

'Please,' Spencer whispered.

Scott struck the soft sand of the beach at a flying run and stumbled. His motion bullied him down to his knees. All he knew was the overpowering dynamo of fear.

As he began to rise, a strange snarling, almost animal in its throatiness, reached his ears. He halted, one arm extended like a branch on a leafless tree.

For that second lightning grazed the sky. In its glare Scott saw a crease of blood stitched across the white beach. He lost caution in his shock.

His head filled with the maniacal snarling, Scott staggered across the beach, following the broken crimson footsteps. They wandered over the dunes with the purposeless instinct of a snail path, though with none of its ease.

The darkness was crushing now, folded over the land like a

sodden blanket. Sand was driving into his face in blinding walls. He shielded his eyes.

There, pausing in the cold and screaming wind, Scott recalled with absolute vision the night that Joseph had fallen onto them from the tree. The sights and sounds of that night seemed part of this. The hoarse rattling growls were no more than an echo of another voice, the smeared trail of blood no more than a reflection from another time. Scott cried out involuntarily and ran on.

Gasping in his haste, he tripped over the first uneven planks of the jetty. He raised his head.

At the very end of the shaking pier Raoul was sitting astride Spencer Hardy's chest. If he was aware of another presence near at hand, he gave no indication of it.

All that Scott recognized of Raoul was the physical. His limbs were inspired by bestial instinct, which blazed in his eyes and knotted his face. The snarling that Scott had heard was coming from Raoul's mouth, bubbling up like vapour from a dark pool of rage. Scott was momentarily hypnotized by the rise and fall of bunched fists, and the rolling tempo of thuds that kept time with the motion.

Raoul was lashing down at Spencer's face, or what remained of it. The inexorable striking of those mindless hands carved now into broken flesh, every blow sinking into the torn and shapeless mask.

It seemed to Scott that the jetty had become a quagmire of blood. Blood was all that featured Spencer Hardy's face: it blackened his body; it slicked Raoul's arms up to the elbows. It welled still from the gory face that stared eyelessly up at Raoul.

Spencer was no longer alive. Scott had no doubt of that. There was a stillness and stiffness to his unresisting body that characterized death. Yet Raoul continued to slam his knuckles down into that empty crimson ball. He continued to beat it from side to side on its slack, spineless neck. He continued to release those terrifying snarls from his frothing mouth.

Scott screamed.

Beyond belief in his own balance, vomiting violently as he did so, Scott reeled across the slippery surface toward Raoul.

He struck him with his momentum as his knees buckled and he slid forward over Spencer's body. Dimly he registered Raoul falling back, clutching at the air. Then there was only red as his face plunged into Spencer's sticky shirt-front.

Seconds later, the snarling filled Scott's ears again. Disbelieving, horrified, he raised his head.

Raoul fell onto him, flailing him with blows. Scott had a brief glimpse of Raoul's face, transformed, as he leaned forward, reaching. His teeth bit into Scott's shoulder.

'Oh, my God,' whispered Scott.

The flesh of his shoulder tore away and Raoul's mouth lunged again. As pain tore through Scott's chest, he moved in the first hesitant reactions of defence. Gripping Raoul's neck in his fingers, he jerked him back, feeling fresh blood spurt from his own wounded chest. Drawing back his hand, he slammed it forward into Raoul's face. Something broke beneath his palm.

Raoul screamed again, a high keening wail, and threw himself forward onto Scott. Hands clawed, teeth tore, knees kicked. As they floundered through the sweet-scented slickness of the jetty, Scott felt himself falling back under this attack.

'Wait,' gasped Scott. 'We must –'

He broke off as Raoul struck him a direct blow, raking the skin from his cheek. His sight swimming, Scott tried to move aside. Raoul's fist connected his nose.

Raoul was onto him, beating and scratching at his eyes. Half-conscious, Scott rolled his head aside. A knee caught him in the groin, and the pain wrenched him into a ball. Raoul pounded his kidneys.

'Raoul,' whispered Scott. 'Raoul, I only want to help you – I – please ...'

In spite of his circumstances, Scott felt the sincerity in himself attuned to the words. There was a deep and unexpected need in his heart – a need far greater than hunger or thirst – to touch something in Raoul. A splintered memory filtered in through his eyes, a memory of Raoul sitting in Scott's bedroom and saying, 'Y'know, Scottie, it's been the best thing of my life to have met you ...'

'Please, Raoul, I swear ... I swear to God that all I want is to be your friend ...'

Raoul fastened his teeth on Scott's throat.

Scott felt sinew tearing away, flesh splitting, beneath that unheeding bite. In a moment, sprawled under Raoul in the oozing slush, writhing with the pain in his throat, Scott knew that his jugular vein was about to be bitten through.

A crack of sound struck them with the force of falling rubble.

Frozen for an instant in this ridiculous – terrible – pose, Scott saw a white bolt cleave the vast well of the skies, web the churning splendour of the clouds, and strike, with unparalleled force, the end of the bluff. His sight fading on a vision of spouting flame, Scott thought numbly, The buds are burnt now. The hanging buds are burnt.

Then – nothing.

The echoes drained away in little tremors under Scott's back. There was a fierce smell of burning in the air.

He was lying down – that much he knew. Jetty and sea below. Sky above. Heavens above. Death ... death ... death ....

This body, stretched beyond limits of pain and endurance. Endurance ... what is the most pain one can endure? A lifetime of pain? An eternity of pain? A season of pain? No pain is endurable. None. But we survive. We survive.

Being aware. Conscious. Having feeling. Having knowledge. Even if only the knowledge of warm wet blood and the beating sea and the smell of burning in the air and ... death ....

Scott opened his eyes. Darkness. Pain.

Lightning charred the sky again, but did not strike the earth. Enough. Raoul was sitting there, next to him, head bowed. He was weeping.

Scott raised his hand to his throat. His fingers felt the solidity of unbroken flesh. For the first time he was aware of the life that trembled beneath his touch. There was something wonderful in the hot pulsing of veins, the thudding of the heart. Scott was washed by a swift wave of euphoria that was as intense as it was out of place in this mad setting of stormy sea and sky. He was drunk with his own existence, afire with the joy of presence, of being. He had followed the rule of life, which was to continue at all costs. Even pain. This rule, the rule the others could not understand. The others who were too evil or too good to survive, who hurt too much inside to go on. Anthony. Raoul.

Scott rolled his head. His thoughts slid and crashed like glass with the force of the movement, and suddenly sadness was there too. He could catch the lingering scent of his terror. This was one of those moments that shaped the world, this moment and all that constituted its substance: the venomous black sea, the babbling wind, the clean white cauldron that was the beach. And more: Raoul, head bowed, hand splashed out rigidly over his hidden face, trembling shudders quivering through his arms and back. Scott closed his eyes and wished that he could lie there forever.

So strange a sight to one who might be looking from above ... or below. Two boys sitting on the edge of a jetty, staring. They are unmoving – well, almost. Apart from an occasional glance at a silent form that lies between them, they do not move. They are still.

'Do you think it will rain tonight?' Scott said.

'Naah.'

Silence. The wind. The waves. The waiting.

'What now, Raoul?'

'I dunno. I dunno.'

'Go back?'

'Naah.'

'It's all over now. It's finished.'

'Yes.'

'It's the end now.'

'Yes. It's finished.'

Scott stared out at the water again. His clothing was wet

with spray as well as blood. It felt as heavy as canvas on him.

'God, Raoul, there must be peace somewhere. We've just got to find it. Maybe if we keep running, far away from other people ....'

'The beach. Let's go down the beach. We must keep near the sea.'

'Yes, let's run! Down the beach, Raoul! For ever. We don't have to be with all this. We can run. Go on, keep on – running. Flying. Away ... above all this ... keep on ... away ... away ....'

Raoul stood up. For a moment he smoothed down his stained costume. Then he turned and started to walk back down the jetty. He reached the sand. Hc turned and shouted back.

'Come, Scottie! Let's go now.'

Scott paused. He could smell the burning still. The burning buds. He rose. With one careless, compassionate foot, he pushed Spencer Hardy off the jetty into the sea. Then he turned and followed Raoul, who was running down the endless beach beside the unquiet water.

'Scottie?'

'Hmm?'

'Don't fall asleep now. You'll trip. We must keep goin'.'

'Mmm.'

'Scottie – I – how long have we been walkin' for?'

'I don't know, Raoul ....'

'How long d'you *think*?'

'Three hours?'

'Christ ... Scottie –'

'What?'

'I dunno really how to say this, but – I – ahh, shit ....'

'Just say it, Raoul.'

'Y'know sometimes when you know just watcha wanna say, but you're too ashamed to talk ... 'cos you know you've been wrong ...? I – feel – that – way – Scott –'

'Don't stop now, Raoul. Talk now. Talk.'

'I can't! I can't say … it.'

'What are you feeling, Raoul?'

'Feelin'? I – dunno. No, I'm lyin', I do, I know … strange.'

'Strange?'

'I'm walkin' on a beach in the dark. Hey, Scott, y'know what I mean … like here I am, an' it's crazy, it's mad – it's nuts! What I am and where I am is nuts, Scott! How can I be here? How can –'

'Don't shout, Raoul, someone will hear.'

'You know where you are, but – like, you can't believe it. Huh, Scottie? It's mad, man, Scott, I – people all over the goddamn world don't know we're here. They couldn't care about us … or anyone else … y'know? Somewhere now, some fat woman in curlers is eatin' grapefruit for breakfast. Maybe it'll squirt juice in her eye an' she'll swear and wipe it, but she won't be thinkin' about you an' me, Scottie. She's never heard of us. She doesn't wanna hear of us. It'll spoil her day.'

'What do you feel about yourself?'

'Myself? You can't really ask that.'

'Why not?'

'Jesus, Scottie, I'm feelin' a million things right now ….'

'Happy?'

'Happy? You – well … sort of, yes.'

'Sort of happy?'

'I said yes, that's right!'

'Don't get angry with me –'

'Well, whaddya want me to say? Listen, I know what I did, Scott, I'm not stupid –'

'You tried to kill me, Raoul.'

'No.'

'Yes, you did. You –'

'I didn't try to, Scott. You just surprised me, that's all. I wasn't expectin' you, I swear!'

'You were biting my throat. Like a dog, or something –'

'I was fightin', I didn't know what I was doin'!'

'Yes, Raoul, all right. What I was really asking you was how does it feel to know that you've murdered somebody?'

'Jesus Christ, Scott, don't be – don't ... look ....'

'How does it feel?'

'He – deserved – it –'

'And you're the judge of that?'

'Don't be stupid, Scott! There's no such thing as judgin' or fairness in this place. We just do things to each other, that's all, we do things because of the way we feel inside, an' we hurt each other ... but we don't judge things! You don't, do you?'

'Yes! Yes .... No – I – maybe you're right, Raoul, after all. Yes. Yes, you are right. I can't judge you.'

'Scottie?'

'What?'

'Arentcha happy too? Walkin' here on the beach? Huh? Nothin's gonna stop us now. We can go on walkin' always.'

'I – yes ... yes, I am happy, Raoul.'

'You an' me are so different ... you're so good, Scottie .. but it was always you an' me, never Joe ...'

'Why did you go to all this trouble for Joseph if you never cared about him?'

'I never said I didn't care, screwball! 'Course I cared. An' I knew that Spencer Hardy had pushed him. I could feel it –'

'Weren't you really feeling something else?'

'Like what, huh?'

'You can answer that.'

'No! No. I've told you before, the only reason was that he pushed Joe! That's all. You were so busy with Anthony Lord that you never even thought about it. Am I right? Am I right, screwball?'

'Anthony and I were friends, Raoul.'

'So were you an' me, Scott.'

'No. No. We weren't, Raoul. You don't know what friendship is, if that's what you think.'

'Bullshit! Crap! You think you an' him had it so hot, huh? Cryin' like a goddamn baby when he died ....'

'That's what I mean by friendship, Raoul.'

'Yes? What was it like? What was so different?'

'When Anthony died, Raoul, there was nothing left here. Nothing.'

'In the world?'

'Nothing.'

'Then tell me this, screwball. Why dintcha follow him?'

'Where?'

'Over the cliff. Why dintcha jump over after him, if you had nothing left? Huh? Why not?'

'But why should –'

''Cos you had nothin' left, you said.'

'Quiet! Be quiet. Don't talk to me.'

'Scottie?'

'What now?'

'Why arentcha talkin' all of a sudden?'

'I'm not ... well, look ... oh, leave it.'

'No, no, tell me, Scottie.'

'I – am ...'

'What? Go on.'

'You're right again. You're right again. I was wrong. There couldn't be nothing left. His death wasn't the absolute end.'

'Well?'

'It did give me something. It gave me pain.'

'What are you –'

'Raoul. Raoul!'

'What? Why are you shakin' like that, Scottie? Are you all right? Are you okay?'

'Raoul – you know why I'm here? Do you know why I came out after you? Do you know why I was sent to Bleda in the first place?'

'Why? Why, Scottie? Get up, please don't lie there, Scottie, please –'

'Because you *are* my friend, Raoul! You *are*! I can't believe it ... what you've done doesn't matter. I meant what I said on the jetty before ... all I ever wanted was to be your friend, Raoul ...'

'Get up, Scott! Don't speak. Don't ... please ....'

'I'm sorry ....'

166

'Sorry? No, Scott ... why should you be sorry? It's me ... who ... what are they going to do with me?'

'Now?'

'For killing him. And all the other things. Are they goin' to hang me, Scott ...?'

'No, no, they won't. You're too young.'

'What, then?'

'They'll send you back to Bleda. That's all.'

'I don't want that, Scott. Not any more. I'd rather die.'

'No, Raoul, remember – it can't be absolute ... there can't be nothing left ....'

'But you're goin' home, Scott. I'll be alone here!'

'You'll have the others, all the others. You'll –'

'But you're the only friend I've got. You don't understand it either, but that's the way it is, Scottie. You're the only thing I can use to get up with now ....'

'Easy, Raoul, go easy ....'

'I killed him, Scott! I took a man in my hands an' I hit him till he died! This blood ... Christ, but he bled! I did it, Scott! It was me! I didn't know that it was in me. What's so different about me? Aren't I the same as you, Scott? Aren't I the same as anyone else?'

'Shhh, yes, you are, Raoul, you are, you are ....'

'Why did I do it, then? How could I have done it?'

'Shh, Raoul, quiet now ....'

'It hurt me, Scott. All this goddamn summer, none of you could see into me, but it hurt. I couldn't think of anything 'cept Spencer Hardy. I wanted to believe that he pushed Joseph, I wanted to believe it ... it was true .... In the beginning, Spencer Hardy was nothin' to me, but I started rememberin' and rememberin' ... and then it all burnt my mind. I dreamed about it. An' it hurt me, Scott. I hurt all the time, I swear it! The things I did ... it hurt me. And all the time I was comin' closer to this ... to tonight ... knowin' what I was gonna do .... But he did push Joe, he must have pushed Joe ... he must have ... Scottie? Scottie .... Is it wrong to hurt inside? Is it a sin to hurt inside? 'Cos that's my only sin, Scottie ... Scottie? Is it a sin to hurt? Scottie ...!'

'Don't cry, Raoul. Please. I can't bear to hear you cry ....'

'Is it a sin, Scottie? Tell me it's not ... please, tell me ... it's not a sin ....'

'It's not a sin, Raoul. It's not sin ....'

'Don't cry, Scottie ... don't cry ....'

'It's so dark, it's so cold ....'

'We must go back now ....'

'I won't leave you, Raoul, I won't leave you ....'

'The storm is still here, but there's no rain. There's never rain....'

'Raoul – Raoul – what's going to happen to us now?'

Dawn soaped down the eastern clouds, spilling suds of light across the grey plane of water. The storm had been lifting for some hours and the wind had starved with it, so the waves were now nothing more than timid insults of foam.

Scott lay on the slope of a high dune. Every joint in his body seemed to be gristled with sand. His sodden clothing fitted him like a wrinkled skin. Beside him, Raoul was a tiny broken figure, stretched out like a mislaid doll.

Scott turned bleary eyes to Raoul's salt-furred face. He was asleep, or nearly so – eyes closed, mouth open. His chest rose and fell in staccato rhythm.

As a long line of birds winged overhead, Scott shifted his gaze up to them. He watched until they had become no more than a thin pencil smudge in the distance before he dropped his chin to his chest.

His weariness was the end result of more than simply a bodily exhaustion: his mind, in reaching a deeper understanding of himself and his circumstances, had drained itself of thought and emotion. He retained now a conscious knowledge that, perhaps, he had always had inside.

He knew who Attila was.

Scott had seen evil in Raoul, but he knew now that there

had been none. He had seen evil *and* suffering in his world, but no longer. There was only suffering.

And – a slow dawning to him – he had realized that, ultimately, there was no real difference between Raoul Dean and Anthony Lord. To each, youth had represented so much more than just the physical masturbation: the act had extended to the state of life itself. Each had been primarily concerned with wringing from every instant of existence the orgasmic fulfilment of the purest emotion, of pleasure, of pain. Yes – each had suffered what to him was nothing less than agony (what is the distinction between bearing the burden of evil and that of good?). Each had been consumed beyond his control in the heat of his own pain. And each – whatever his motive – had after all denied the moth its passage to the light.

This, then, was Attila in Scott's eyes: the corroding, unchanging, faceless suffering of the human heart.

Scott sat up as Raoul stirred. They did not speak. Water clapped the sand with bony hands.

'Are we far from Bleda still?' Raoul said, then started as he looked up.

The bluff lay like a tarry wing a kilometre down the beach. Even from where they lay, the individual windows of the reformatory building could be distinguished in the grey stone.

'No bars now,' Scott murmured as he rose, aching through to his innermost flesh.

The tower light, pale in the face of the sun, beckoned them on across the sand.

There is a large crowd standing on the lawns when Raoul and Scott come up the path. The boys from their dormitory are there. The police are there. Mr Bishop is there. Dr Berry is there.

Scott sees his father, but nothing moves inside him. He is surprised – he expected something to happen. A twinge of guilt, maybe.

Dr Berry looks older somehow; his hair is thinner. Oh, but

then it was falling out fast even before Scott left. His skin too –
paler. Tighter. Maybe just from a sleepless night waiting for
his son to return. Maybe from worrying about all the patients
he should have been examining right then.

Scott wants to talk to him, but he can't think of anything to
say. As he and Raoul walk up the path towards the people,
they draw back and stare as though the two youths are naked.
There is silence.

Scott stops as he reaches level ground, but Raoul moves unhesitatingly forward. He goes up to Mr Bishop and halts.

'I have killed Spencer Hardy,' he says.

So that is how he decided to do it, Scott thinks. He has been
wondering how it would be done. But it's better like this, better by far. No delay.

A woman standing next to Mr Bishop faints. There is something familiar in her features. Then Scott realizes – she is
Spencer Hardy's mother.

Foolish woman, Scott thinks. Foolish. Foolish to cry out in
joy as she passed the infant from her belly, squealing, into the
light. Foolish to urge and praise and cajole and tease and love
through all the years of pain. Foolish to hope. Foolish to faint
when she hears that he lives no longer.

Nevertheless, Scott feels bad. He feels bad for this unknown woman who lies pale and cold on the ground. He
wants to comfort her. He feels bad while she is surrounded
and revived and consoled; he feels bad while she is carried
away to the matron's room.

He feels bad while Raoul is forced to answer questions. He
feels bad while Mr Bishop screams and raves as he hears the
story, and then raises a hand to strike Raoul's cheek. He still
feels bad as two policemen order Raoul to go upstairs and
pack his bags.

Scott begins to follow Raoul through the press of bodies but
then he pushes past and hurries ahead of him. So it happens
that he has climbed the twisting stairs, walked the soft floor of
the passage, and is sitting in the dormitory when Raoul finally
comes in to start packing.

Raoul is obviously suppressing tears as he goes over to his locker. His cheek is red where Mr Bishop has struck him.

Scott wants to fly with him beyond forever, but he knows he cannot. Yet.

Scott crosses to his bed. With two calm hands he hurls the mattress to the floor. There is something flattened across the springs. He picks it up and holds it across his chest. Raoul looks at it.

It is a black shirt with a piece torn from it.

'You?' cries Raoul.

Scott says nothing. There is nothing to say. He lets the shirt fall to the floor, then turns and walks to the window. The stone is warm beneath his fingers.

Scott has told Raoul that he will never leave him, but the choice, now, is Raoul's. And Raoul knows it. If he says nothing to anybody about the black garment, then Scott is free. Free to find his chains. If he tells what he knows, then Scott will be with Raoul for ever. Free also – in spite of bars – because they are friends. And that is all that matters.

Raoul stares at Scott, aghast.

But Scott is looking out of the window, at the waves. He is waiting for Raoul to make his choice.

The sea, today, is calm too. Scott sees something of himself, perhaps – of man – in this eternal animal; sees his own enduring substance in the crying of the water on the rocks; in the peace of the sleeping depths; in all the rage and quietness of the foam.

'Why, Scottie? Why?'

Scott relives for one ghastly minute the fragmentation of his soul as he propelled Joseph from the brink. He lives, too, that deeper level of pain. The years and years of possessing jealousy, his violent resentment of Joseph, his own fanatical devotion to Raoul. He tastes the bitter culmination of fury as he sees Joseph's figure against the cliff edge and knows the opportunity for a life alone with the one person he has been unable to leave behind through time. Raoul. But in the end, it all comes back to the pain: the pain inside. That is the only 'why' that is important.

The crowd below has gone. Only Dr Berry is left, standing idly in the sun. He looks at his watch. Scott wonders whether he will go back to his office now and return to fetch him at lunchtime. It is most likely he will; his patients pay him well. What will he find when he returns?

Raoul has almost reached his decision. He is crying openly now, crying as he thinks of Joseph flying through the air.

But Scott grips the stone and yearns: this moment forever in time. Give to us the breaking sea. The old regret. The promised peace.

Dr Berry begins to walk towards his car. Scott smiles.

MORE ABOUT PENGUINS, PELICANS AND PUFFINS

For further information about books available from Penguins please write to Dept EP, Penguin Books Ltd, Harmondsworth, Middlesex UB7 0DA.

In the U.S.A.: For a complete list of books available from Penguins in the United States write to Dept DG, Penguin Books, 299 Murray Hill Parkway, East Rutherford, New Jersey 07073.

In Canada: For a complete list of books available from Penguins in Canada write to Penguin Books Canada Ltd, 2801 John Street, Markham, Ontario L3R 1B4.

In Australia: For a complete list of books available from Penguins in Australia write to the Marketing Department, Penguin Books Australia Ltd, P.O. Box 257, Ringwood, Victoria 3134.

In New Zealand: For a complete list of books available from Penguins in New Zealand write to the Marketing Department, Penguin Books (N.Z.) Ltd, P.O. Box 4019, Auckland 10.

In India: For a complete list of books available from Penguins in India write to Penguin Overseas Ltd, 706 Eros Apartments, 56 Nehru Place, New Delhi 110019.

TSOTSI
Athol Fugard

'An engrossing psychological thriller which is certainly one of the best novels in South African fiction' – *The Times Literary Supplement*

Tsotsi is a white man's version of the black ghetto, seen with nightmare clarity.

In the shadows of Sophiatown in South Africa stalks Tsotsi, the gangster, bringing pain and terror. Derelict, deprived, nihilistic, he treats life as it has treated him until a chance encounter with a woman leaves him holding a life in his hands: and into the parched and agonized territory of Tsotsi's soul is born a strange redemption.

Written twenty years ago by Fugard, the world-famous dramatist, *Tsotsi* has only recently been published. It is a novel as timeless and terrible in its portrayal of injustice as *Cry, the Beloved Country*.

IN A PROVINCE
Laurens van der Post

Leaving the kraal and the misty Valley of a Thousand Hills, Kenon has come to Port Benjamin in search of work. In Johan he finds a master – and a friend. For a time it seems that their unorthodox friendship can break down the traditional barrier between black and white. But storm clouds are gathering, conflicting forces of love and politics that will explode into tragedy.

In a Province was Laurens van der Post's first novel, written with a young man's fire and fury, but tempered by his characteristic wisdom and the profound human understanding that have made it a small classic in its treatment of racial conflict in Africa.

DUSKLANDS

A specialist in psychological warfare is driven by the stresses of a project for mass destruction in Vietnam to commit an act of obscene violence which violates every principle of humanity.

A megalomaniac Boer takes his bloody revenge on the Hottentot tribe who have humiliated him, journeying as he does so into new territories ripe for colonization.

Together these men represent a paradox of chilling extremes – for as they push back the frontiers of knowledge so too do they assist at the death of the spirit.

Dusklands was J. M. Coetzee's first work of fiction, and in these two novellas he distils the absurdity and horror of scientific evangelism and heroic exploration united in a terrible marriage of destruction.

'J. M. Coetzee's vision goes to the nerve-centre of being. What he finds there is more than most people will ever know about themselves' – Nadine Gordimer

WAITING FOR THE BARBARIANS

For decades the Magistrate has run the affairs of a tiny frontier settlement, ignoring the impending war between the barbarians and the Empire, whose servant he is. But when the interrogation experts arrive, he is jolted into sympathy with the victims and into a quixotic act of rebellion which lands him in prison, branded as an enemy of the state.

J. M. Coetzee's second prize-winning novel is an allegory of oppressor and oppressed. Not simply a man living through a crisis of conscience in an obscure place in remote times, the Magistrate is an analogue of all men living in complicity with regimes that ignore justice and decency.

'A remarkable and original book' – Graham Greene

'I have known few authors who can evoke such a wilderness in the heart of man ... Mr Coetzee knows the elusive terror of Kafka' – Bernard Levin

Nadine Gordimer in Penguins

JULY'S PEOPLE

For years, it has been what is called a 'deteriorating situation'. Now it is war: all over South Africa the cities are battlegrounds. Bam and Maureen Smales – enlightened, liberal whites – are rescued from the terror by their servant, July, who leads them and their three children to refuge in his native village. What happens to the Smales, and to July, mirrors the changes in the world at large: the shifts in character and relationships give us an unforgettable look into the terrifying, tacit understandings between black and white.

'This is the best novel that Miss Gordimer has ever written' – Alan Paton in the *Saturday Review*

SIX FEET OF THE COUNTRY

'Gordimer's setting is Africa . . . but in her Africa, we find ourselves' – *Washington Post*

Seven stories from South Africa's finest writer that distil the essence of what has been happening in that country in recent years, through people and landscapes so intensely and evocatively drawn that they seem to burn a hole in the page.

'Sensuous, witty, wise . . . her qualities need no inventory from me' – Christopher Wordsworth in the *Guardian*

'To read her is to discover Africa's realities' – Paul Theroux in the *New Statesman*

The stories included here have been selected from two previous collections, *No Place Like* and *A Soldier's Embrace*.

William Boyd in Penguins

AN ICE-CREAM WAR

As millions are slaughtered on the Western Front, a ridiculous and little remarked-on campaign is being waged in East Africa – a war that continued after the Armistice because no one told them to stop.

Primarily a gripping story of the men and women swept up by the passions of love and battle, William Boyd's magnificently entertaining novel also elicits the cruel futility and tragedy of it all.

'A towering achievement' – John Carey, Chairman of the Booker Prize Judges 1982

'Quite outstanding' – *Sunday Times*

'If you can imagine John Buchan or Rider Haggard rewritten by Evelyn Waugh then you have something of the flavour of this book . . . Very funny' – Robert Nye in the *Guardian*

A GOOD MAN IN AFRICA

Morgan Leafy isn't overburdened with worldly success. Actually, he is refreshingly free from it. But then, as a representative of Her Britannic Majesty in tropical Kinjanja, it was not very constructive of him to get involved in wholesale bribery and with sensitive local politicians. Nor was it exactly oiling his way up the ladder to hunt down the improbably pointed breasts of his boss's daughter when officially banned from horizontal delights by a nasty dose . . .

Falling back on his deep-laid reserves of misanthropy and guile, Morgan has to fight off the sea of humiliation, betrayal and *ju-ju* that threatens to wash over him.

'Wickedly funny' – *The Times*

'Splendid rollicking stuff!' – *Spectator*

Winner of a 1981 Whitbread Literary Award

Winner of the 1982 Somerset Maugham Award

CHANGING PLACES

The plate-glass, concrete jungle of Euphoria State University, USA, and the damp red-brick University of Rummidge have an annual exchange scheme. Normally the exchange passes without comment.

But when Philip Swallow swaps with Professor Zapp the fates play a hand, and the two academics find themselves enmeshed in a spiralling involvement on opposite sides of the Atlantic. Nobody is immune: students, colleagues, even wives are swapped as the tension increases. Finally, the cat is let out of the bag with a flourish that surprises even the author himself.

'Three star rating for a laugh a line' – Auberon Waugh in the *Evening Standard*

'By far the funniest novel of the year ... the cool, cruel detachment of Evelyn Waugh' – *Daily Mail*

Winner of the Hawthornden Prize and the *Yorkshire Post* fiction prize

HOW FAR CAN YOU GO?

How far could they go? On one hand there was the traditional Catholic Church, on the other the siren call of the permissive society. And what with the advent of COC (Catholics for an Open Church), the social lubrication of the Pill and the disappearance of Hell, it was difficult for Polly, Dennis, Angela and the others not to rupture their spiritual virginity on the way to the seventies ...

'Hilarious ... a magnificent book' – Graham Greene

'Huge, bitterly funny and superbly presented montage of the false nostrums that assailed Christianity like worms' – *Sunday Times*

Winner of the Whitbread Book of the Year Award

and

THE BRITISH MUSEUM IS FALLING DOWN

SHUTTLECOCK

Prentis, senior clerk in the 'dead crimes' department of police archives, is becoming more and more paranoiac ... Alienated from his wife and children, and obsessed by his father, a wartime hero now the mute inmate of a mental hospital, Prentis feels increasingly unsettled as his enigmatic boss Mr Quinn turns his investigations towards himself – and his father ...

'An astonishing study of forms of guilt, laced with a thread of detection, and puckering now and then into outrageous humour' – *Sunday Times*

THE SWEET-SHOP OWNER

A symbol, a token of life, an attitude ... the sweet shop was all that and more. It was the bargain struck between Chapman and his beautiful, ailing, depressive wife. Safely penned up amongst its confectionary and newspapers, Chapman was defused as a threat to her, impotently confined to stocktaking and reorders.

It was a bargain, strangely enough, based on love and courageous acceptance of life's deprivations ... threatened only by Dorry, their clever, angry daughter who will never forgive either of them.

'A marvellous first novel' – *New Statesman*

THE HEALING ART

Winner of the Somerset Maugham Award, the Southern Arts Literature Prize and the Arts Council National Book Award

Pamela Cowper is facing death. Not a vague probability, but a shockingly imminent oblivion from cancer. How will she face it?

Dorothy Higgs, on the other hand, is told that she will live to be one of her doctor's success stories. And, as the two women confront their destinies across the gulfs of fear and hope, fate, as always, reserves the final twist until the end.

'Not a page goes by without our being astounded' – John Braine in the *Sunday Telegraph*

'I could never have enough of it' – Auberon Waugh in the *Evening Standard*

WHO WAS OSWALD FISH?

Well, who *was* Oswald Fish? Find out in this novel that froths and hums with Rabelaisian farce and rumbustious sex ... a book that William Boyd has described as 'the comic novel at its most mature and impressive: an amused and entertaining – but at the core, serious – commentary on the vanities and pretensions of the human condition'.

'A. N. Wilson is a master at playing black comedy that can make us laugh just when we should cry' – *New Statesman*

and

THE SWEETS OF PIMLICO
WISE VIRGIN

OH WHAT A PARADISE IT SEEMS
John Cheever

Skating on Beasley's Pond always makes Lemuel Sears feel nostalgic. He is old enough to wonder – after skating, or when he sees a young couple kissing in the cinema – whether sometime soon he will be exiled from the pleasures of love.

Meanwhile, there is Renée. He first noticed Renée, her style, her splendid and endearing figure, in a New York bank. With her, even in polluted, fast-food, nomad America, the illusion of Paradise lingers. Until he returns to find his free skating rink turned into a municipal dump. And until . . . But Renée has always said, 'You don't understand the first thing about women.'

GINGER, YOU'RE BARMY
David Lodge

When it isn't prison, it's hell.

Or that's the heartfelt belief of conscripts Jonathan Browne and Mike 'Ginger' Brady. For this is the British Army in the days of National Service, a grimy deposit of post-war cynicism, it consists of one endless, shambling round of kit layout, square-bashing, shepherd's pie 'made from real shepherds', P.T. and drill relieved by the occasional lecture on firearms or V.D. The reckless, impulsive Mike and the more pragmatic Jonathan adopt radically different attitudes to this two-year confiscation of their freedom . . . and the consequences are dramatic.

MONSIGNOR QUIXOTE
Graham Greene

A wonderfully picaresque and profoundly moving tale of innocence at large amidst the shrines and fleshpots of modern Spain, Graham Green's novel, like Cervantes's seventeenth-century classic, is also a brilliant fable for our times.

'A deliciously funny novel and an affectionate offering to all that is noblest and least changing in the people and life of Spain' – Michael Ratcliffe in *The Times*

HEADBIRTHS
Günter Grass

Should Dörte and Harm Peters – today's quintessential German couple – have a baby?

Formidably gifted, funny and wise, Günter Grass whisks us off on a fact-finding holiday with the Peters, to the sprawling teeming slums of Asia where (true liberals) they contemplate the population explosion, world poverty, nuclear war ... yes-to-baby, no-to-baby? And where, in a novel stuffed with fantastic 'headbirths' and outrageous invention, Günter Grass probes the modern German psyche with his own special brand of brilliant and devastating wit.

'Part novel, part film script, part essay, part soliloquy ... Grass is a playful, exuberant, amazing writer' – Paul Bailey in the *Standard*